The Acrophile

Yoram Kaniuk

The

ACROPHILE

Translated from the Hebrew
by Zeva Shapiro

New York

Atheneum Publishers

1961

The Acrophile

My wife left at the end of the spring. I remained alone in the city, chained to the new season like an eye fixed at a keyhole, peering, intent. Countless evenings choked with heat merged with one another. Their meaning: heavy indolence of days with no beginning. Unlike spring—when day yearns for dusk—these were tired days. Nights filled with the noises of neighborhood: steel fire escapes, the iron steps of decaying New York brownstones littered with people, discarded beer cans toppling unheeded to the pavement, radios, trucks shifting gears directly below the window before disappearing into the huge cavern beneath the river. Summer, a presence sensed more than seen, strangled by the New York sun—not so much by its ponderous heat as by dankness—stagnant, oppressive. It was difficult to study. Even more difficult was the wish to study.

I was about to get my degree and planned to send the certificate to my mother. She would hang it with the others above my father's bookcase where they could smile at each other, my mother at the degrees, the degrees at my mother. "From kindergarten to advanced degree."

There are people shorter than I; still, the fact that I am small, which relates to the defiant line of my brow, is an aspect of my identity. My face, not distinctly handsome, is—at least to those not too occupied with themselves to express an opinion, as well as to myself—pleasant enough. Regarded from my perspective, the weather is not as a tall person might see it, floating high, pure and blue; I see it stretched out before me, intimate, enveloped in dust. If one were to line up the diplomas above my father's bookcase, the row would be many times longer than I am. Diplomas can be stored along with the memory of all the meals you have eaten; whereas your height is always with you. . . .

My wife was on the road. She went from city to city playing the role of an old flower vendor, a symbol of death. She wore a black shroud; death glared in her eyes—she played death and was expected to live the part. Each night she died in another city whose name she hardly remembered; once in Cincinnati, with the next morning's breakfast in Akron, Ohio; another time waking from a dream of death to die in Indiana. When she was lonely she would call me on the phone. But this was no consolation— a woman on the other end of the wire who wants to be told how much you miss her; how empty New York is; that night and day you think only of her; and incidentally, have you seen Sarah-John-Alex-Phyllis-Horace? It is a raucous summer night; how can you think of what is missing when you can't bear what you have?

I would sometimes call her. It once happened that we called each other at the same time. After five minutes I began to think of the expense and wanted to end the conversation. "I'm wasting money," I said to her. "Wasting?" "Not wasting, spending." "Not you, it's I who am spending it," she snapped. "Not only do I call, I also pay. Not only do I pay, but I have to put up with your complaints. You ought to be ashamed." "Ashamed? It was I who made the call. . . ." "No, it wasn't, I made the call and you're crying." "Crying? Who's crying?" And so on, until finally we were both laughing.

"See," she said. "It's fate—we were thinking of each other, at exactly the same moment. It happens that way with lovers. . . ."

She believed in fate, fortunetelling, divination, ghosts, good-luck charms—all things supernatural. Wherever she went she would visit palm readers, and devour the messages in Chinese fortune cookies. In Dallas that summer she went to see a gypsy fortuneteller.

"The gypsy," my wife used to say to me, "gazes at her blue crystal ball just as you or I would; we see the trees, whereas she sees the forest—the forest has its own logic. The crystal is the essence of sea gathered up in the palm of a hand. With each breath, she draws in its great roaring silence; she regards the tides, the waves advancing through her bosom, receding. . . . Her soul, once glass, is transformed with a gesture, a mirror which captures a fleeting vision and encloses it—all of eternity in a small crystal sphere."

My wife continued: "Her soul is borne into the vast unknown on flakes of crystal. The sea contracts. The ocean's clamor is reduced to a slight bird cry. She looks back and sees me climbing a mountain. She rests at the peak and waits—like David, the painter, waiting before the smooth blank canvas, to see the picture hidden in his heart—the future pictured in his soul: two pigeons pulling golden threads, swimming slowly into space and endless time, filling it with secret beauty. David the painter, careless, allows the picture to sneak onto the canvas. Don't laugh, Professor, you can study two whole centuries, but you won't discover the cause—the why of sea shells, engraved, carved, finished with a grandeur beyond the power of any artist, resting at the ocean bottom where no eye can possess them."

"I know," I told her. She didn't believe me and I made no attempt to explain.

The Dallas gypsy was upset when she gazed into her crystal ball.

"What is your name, my child?"

"Mira. From New York," she added out of habit.

"You have a family?"

"Yes."

"Your mother's dead?"

"No, she's alive," Mira said.

The gypsy fell into a long silence. "You're certain?" she asked.

"Of course I'm certain. Just a week ago my father wrote that . . . no, no, she's not going to die!"

The gypsy interrupted in a somber voice: "We will all die."

My wife smiled sullenly and began to pick the nail of her right thumb.

"I see a bridge," the gypsy continued. "An old wooden bridge, decayed by sun and rain." She raised her voice and looked at Mira with compassion, then withdrew, becoming remote and impassive, like a telegraph wire, indifferent to the message it transmits. "Did your father love your mother?" she asked suddenly. Mira mumbled a reply. "You'll swallow your finger," the gypsy smiled through two ugly gold teeth, and tapped her hand gently.

"An old woman, small, wrinkled, is standing on the crumbling bridge; black wood crashes with a clamor that fades and wells up again as from some deep spring. The woman's face is innocent—the innocence of things being one with their hidden guile. She holds a baby: your mother. She holds her for a moment fixed in time by a pin, then lets go. The baby tumbles, at first slowly, then swift and hard. The earth parts its lips and speaks: 'Thank you, damned witch, you shall be blessed.' The baby, its face wreathed in smiles, is devoured."

The gyspy looked up at my wife, exultant. "She was received by the restful earth. . . ."

"Stop it!" my wife shrieked. "I don't believe you. I don't believe a word. Mother is alive."

"It's good that you don't believe it," the gypsy said dolefully. "Two dollars. Bad news, two dollars; good news, one. People come to hear the bad, not the good."

Mira paid and left. That night she called me.

When I picked up the phone she was crying.

"My mother is sick and you didn't tell me."

"That's a lie," I protested.

"No, it's true. The gypsy told me."

I tried to change the subject, but it was no use.

"I know she's sick," Mira said, "and you're all hiding it from me. I paid the gypsy two dollars. Had I paid her one, I would now be laughing."

"She is sick, but it's not very serious," I lied. "We didn't want to worry you. By the time you're back, she'll be well enough to stroll down Fifth Avenue with you, laughing at the world."

"The world isn't so funny," my wife said bitterly.

"Mira, be patient. You'll come to New York with the show and be a big hit. Your mother will sit in the first row, applauding. Don't waste all the years of hard work."

"You never did understand very much," she said, "and you have no heart, so it's no use explaining things to you. Goodbye."

Next night she was back, somewhat pale, but lovely. Patches of flesh, tanned by the southern sun, showed through her flimsy green dress. She was

thinner, yet animated. As soon as she arrived we
went to her parents' home.

It was early autumn. The first signs of the season
could be seen, treading softly, groping, not quite
touching, as New York, august metropolis, shook
off the last traces of summer from its languid limbs,
and standing firm, painted its own horizon with a
single distracted brush stroke. The skies, flushed
with the shame of this display, took on a vivid
twilight which descended like soft whistling. . . .
The air was pure and clear as the evening, which
embraced it and lit the street lights all at once in
its honor. All at once, lit and quenched, the lights
made flickering darkness. A new world was en-
kindled in the spreading night.

Morris Zucker, my father-in-law, opened the
door. He was not well to do, yet his clothes were
extravagant. A flashy handkerchief always adorned

his jacket pocket. He fell on my wife and kissed her again and again with deep emotion (my father-in-law wore emotions as others wear clothes), tears streaming down his cheeks. Suddenly, as if remembering something, he excused himself and directed us to the other room. My wife went quickly. I followed her, found myself a spot in the corner, and looked out at the room which was seeing itself through my eyes, so that we were strangers.

You marry a girl, and with her comes an entire estate: father, mother, breakfast smells, the train she used to take to school, the beautiful flower gardens she dreamed of on cold nights—so you build yourself a wall. Mostly you live at a distance from her. You build your own world and that's it. Suddenly comes mourning, someone is about to die. You are confronted: family, breakfast smells, flowers. . . . You had taken care to build a wall, but the wall turns to paper and burns.

I remained in the corner because I hate emotional scenes. They make me feel alone, also homesick. I come from a faraway place. There in Israel, along a sun-drenched road, beyond a fence of thorns, I have a mother and father and rooms full of memories. It embarrasses me to be homesick.

I wanted to break through the wall, but it stood immobile, leering at me. I saw my wife—thousands of miles away, yet only two steps off. She was watching her mother who lay in an extravagant double bed, reeking of death. Drop by drop, each moment a year of living, her life ebbed away. Deep inside perhaps she still belonged to the world, to the outside noises, the ticking of clocks. But her body was inert and her face like the midsummer fields of the valley of Jezreel: dark patches, furrows, less stone than dry, despondent earth; a broad vista seared by *hamsin* winds that crave water; sharp tracks of a plough fading with the faded yellow stalks that cling vainly to unyielding soil.

Mrs. Zucker, my mother-in-law, had, in her youth, been more than life itself—a challenge to the heart of night, an endless chain of activity, force, devotion and excitement. Mrs. Zucker, my mother-in-law, lay in her voluptuous bed and was no longer growing. The idea possessed me: when one is going, he must go somewhere; when one grows, where to? A person grows and grows, and when he's finished, dies. I almost laughed. A woman sixty years old, more dead than alive, and the meaning of it: she's stopped growing.

"They're all here," she mumbled, and there was a hush in the room. "Mira, Abe, Morris, Adele." She omitted my name. To Mrs. Zucker, her daughter, my wife, would always be the young virgin upon whom she pronounced fervent blessings, and for whose sake she kept a faded blossom beneath her pillow. She had never pretended to like me.

"Now that you're all here, I can go. I couldn't go without saying goodbye. How nice it is to see you all," she said, attempting to raise herself on the pillow. "The main thing is to scream," she stammered. "If you scream no one will ask any questions. Always scream, and you'll always win. Ha-ha-ha."

The cynical overtone of her laugh was hardly appropriate. "I've done a good deal of screaming in my day." Her voice was steady now. "I was a wild young thing. Remember, Mira? No, you couldn't possibly remember. You were still in my stomach then. We were at the zoo. Everyone was watching the elephants, but I was fascinated by one particular goat, a young one, who was trying to leap. He couldn't get off the ground at all, poor thing. I'm like him. Something is always in the way."

She paused and then continued with excitement. "Hello there. They can't see you. They see only with their eyes. I—with my entire soul. I see a giant halo. A bridal canopy, cruel, self-contained. . . ." She was almost shouting. "A halo, not man, not woman, neither angels nor archangels come to me now. . . . My halo is coming."

This is what my mother-in-law, Mrs. Zucker, said on her lavish deathbed. "A simple halo. No, there's no such thing. Nothing, for that matter, is simple. You, sister of fate, asking me to come quietly, like a maiden—I shall, I promise. All the screaming, the noise of my life, did me no good. I have left no mark. Take me, my sweet halo. I am tired of watching you."

She fell back on her pillow, a vacant smile il-luminating her face. My wife flung herself on the bloated body of her mother, who was breathing heavily now, in a short noisy whistle. I left the room and found my father-in-law, Morris, talking on the phone. He was inviting Steven Scott, our handsome violinist friend, to play at his wife's funeral. Mr. Zucker screamed, irritated, "I don't know when. Tomorrow, the next day, I don't know. She always loved your playing. She thought so well of you. She will be happy, she will be happy to hear you."

He hung up the phone briskly, sat down and lit a cigarette. Watching him, I began to think back to when I first knew my wife's family. I was thinking of that time not too long ago when I first met Mira.

My entire being then was bent on work. I was shut in my room; life and I were not enemies, but forgotten friends.

I occupied a furnished room for which I paid eight dollars a week, and like one entombed in the bowels of the earth, I seldom saw light. I was estranged, friendless, yet my heart grieved not at all.

One day, the first of spring by the calendar and habits of this land, and happily a spring day as well, God, as if heedful of the pleas of his creatures grappling with the long winter, was moved to unfold an unblemished sky and warm the city. Looking up at the clear sky with surprise, people smiled at each other, unbuttoned their coats and were like children in a dream.

I found myself outdoors, and approaching the park where painters were sketching spring in colored chalk on the path beside the fountain, I watched them. The jasmine smells of childhood wafted through mind and memory.

A young girl's eyes caught my attention. She was sitting with friends who amused themselves at the expense of the earnest painters. Answering to her eyes, like those of a child sucking a sweet, I smiled at her. She smiled back and twinkled the brown toe that peered out of a sandal. One of her friends, a solemn girl wearing her father's countenance as part of her makeup, said, "Who are you?" Answering to the brown toe, which, now smiled brazenly at me, I said, "As our smiles have already met, I will follow them up by introducing myself. My name is Daan."

"He is a foreigner," said the third girl, who was looking for gold in her nose, digging fiercely.

"I am created in God's image," I said. At this they all laughed.

The young girl's name was Mira. Mira had a strange ageless look; in her spring and winter joined hands. She had proud white teeth and a sweet boyish face crowned with short black hair. She asked me questions which followed each other rapidly and without hesitation.

"Why don't you like barbers?"

"I love them."

"Are you afraid of them?"

"I'm terrified, but sometimes I'm brave, and afterwards I always catch cold."

"You have a very handsome forehead; you shouldn't hide it. You look like a corpse on a day off."

"I'm happy. I like you too."

"You don't, but you will. Do you believe in magic?"

"Well . . ."

"You should. The whole world is made of magic. It takes a million disconnected magics, interwoven in secret and complex design, to produce such a meeting as yours and mine."

"That's nonsense!"

"I knew you would say that."

"I knew you knew."

"You're nice. You should buy yourself some new clothes."

"You're right."

"I'm always right."

"Even a clock that has stopped is right twice a day."

"What are you, a teacher at the school there?" She pointed to the large university across the way.

"No, I study and do research."

"In what?"

"The language of the black cave people and its relation to the Indo-European family of languages."

"That sounds screwy, but it will do."

This was the mode of our conversation, both of us being spring-struck, and unguarded. Her two girl friends having departed, the painters having adjourned to their evening haunts, we were alone in the park.

It was dusk; the warmth of day routed by evening chill, the air now hovered in motion, yet no longer weighed heavily on one's neck as in winter. I put my arm in hers and she leaned her head on my chest. Her ageless look fluttered and settled; she was an eager child.

"A day off from kindergarten," I said, to which she said without a smile, "Yes. Maybe you would be my mommydaddy, please?"

"Yes."

"Are there many skeletons in your black caves?"

"I've never been to them," I said. "I speculate from books and papers. I only theorize; that's fun, and tidy."

"I am happy," she said, "as long as you are one yourself."

"A skeleton?"

"Yes—holding up a man."

We walked, she nibbling me with warm words;

I, proud with pleasure, being unaccustomed to woman's ways.

We went into a restaurant, still drunk from our sudden closeness. We couldn't eat, and drank coffee after coffee. She told me she was an actress and told me about the theatre. It was strange to her that though I considered myself an educated man I had never been to the theatre, not since a production I saw as a child.

At one point I burned my fingers while trying to light a cigarette; a sugar wrapper caught the fire and Mira was amused, for I was flustered and hung my head like a scolded dog. Her laugh was fresh and open like those half-forgotten memories of childhood, and I became aware that for the first time in years I craved something real, simple, with flesh on. I asked her if she would come to my room. "Yes," she said, "for I love you, now that you have given me your hurt and I have given you my laughter." She crooked her little finger into mine and we left.

My room was a few streets away. We walked slowly. My foot was sore. A nail had stuck in my heel and though it was removed, I still felt pain. I've always been prone to magnify pain because I think of my body as a suitcase carrying an important document, the safety of which demands a perfect carrier.

We reached my room, and she laughed. I asked, "Why are you laughing?"

She said, "I'm laughing because the oddest-looking creature I've ever seen, wearing the shabbiest coat, limping like an old horse, lives in a room altogether the size of an olive."

Seeing my room through her eyes, I too laughed. Its most notable feature, the window, occupied almost the entire wall, every one of its panes recalling a different building season. The plaster hung on the ceiling like a bandage on an ancient warrior. We were enjoying the spectacle of the room when suddenly, as it does every five minutes, the subway roared by a few levels below. The room went mad: windows rattled, the table tottered, bed springs rocked, the ceiling shed a patch of plaster, the rubbish pile quivered.

Mira went to the window, which looked into a court lined on four sides by buildings, where it was the local custom to dump refuse, beer cans and dirty water, charging the air with a stench matched only in hell. On rare occasions when the window was open, particularly in summer, when only air could sweeten life in my tiny cell, I would think of dead mice.

Opening the window, what was left for me but to string myself on the laundry line extending above this uncourtly courtyard, and crow like a hapless rooster cock-a-doodle-do to the lord of the universe who has forgotten my name?

Mira was quick to make friends with my room, and amid laughter over the cigarette butts, papers, textbooks and clothes which littered its surface, took an old broom that had been sleeping in a corner and started cleaning. She was fast and thorough, and when she finished lectured me about the hazards of unclean rooms, mice and the plague.

Then she set herself down near the window, stared into the yard, and her smile was gone. She told me she was going to take care of me, and bring order into my life. I came and stood behind her and breathed her hair. I bent and kissed her. She was still.

"Did you ever tell someone you loved her?" she asked.

"Long ago," I said, "I hid the key to my heart in a dark place and I have forgotten where it is."

"That's a challenge," she said, and she turned around and kissed my nose. "My father loves everyone," she said, musing, "and he tells them so." Then opening her voice she said, "When you talked about your black caves before, you were passionate, yet you pick me up in the park, take me to your home, and are not passionate about me at all. No, don't say anything. You see, if I want to be happy I must stick to you, first to make you passionate and win you over, then, to make you strong, I will lose to you. You see, I can fight as hard to lose as other people fight to win." I kissed her again.

"You're funny," she said, and laughed. "I love

you madly, but why, for God's sake, why? Tomorrow I will not see you. If you call me tomorrow, I will not talk to you."

"But I never call anyone," I said.

"In that case I'll come here," she said.

At five in the morning I took her home. Before I left her she kissed my nose again, gently, a butterfly kiss.

When I returned, I found my room had been robbed, plundered.

Why, in a city of elegant homes, flowing with money, jewels, gold and silver, why was my room chosen? Consider yourself a pauper, as I have always done, and you may suddenly discover that the contrary is true. Someone absconds with your possessions and you, who think yourself of no means, learn otherwise. I wonder how the culprits ever found my room. The entire floor was once one apartment and now, out of this glorious memory, endless rooms have been carved. It seemed to me that every time our landlord came back from his annual trips to the good sun of Florida, he would terrify the superintendent into splitting the labyrinth cell block into still smaller cubicles, and while he was at it, raise the rent. A spacious room with a bath could at one time be had for six dollars a week, whereas my present room, which had been the additional bath, hidden between what was once a coatroom and the space under the stairs, now cost eight dollars a week, with two weeks in advance. One had to be either an archeologist or a prophet to find where my room was and how to get into it. From this hidden masterpiece, this vacuum, the thieves had seized an electric plate, a kettle, glasses, two cups, an iron that whistled, ten precious books, an alarm clock, a radio, pipes, ten dollars in cash, a bottle of wine, a typewriter and a fountain pen. After I calculated all that was gone I estimated my loss at one hundred and fifty dollars.

The next evening, Mira asked me to marry her and I agreed. For I had suffered a capital loss, and it seemed to me that a man who could be robbed of one hundred and fifty dollars could surely support a wife. Besides, Mira was doing fairly well as an actress. As for me, being totally devoted to my studies, I paid no attention to my room.

Mira told her parents of our plan. After surveying me from every angle, they granted their consent, albeit none too eagerly.

A few days later I found myself here, in the house of my betrothed, where everyone was astir with preparations for the wedding. Though all the activity was on my behalf, having been assigned no task, and having no friends of my own to invite, I stood alone—an intruder. The others, sprawled on the couch, squatting on the rug, hunched close to the table, pored diligently over their lists.

From the moment we met, it had been Mira's resolve: I was to be HERS. Nothing remained of me beyond those four letters. I was no longer my mother's beloved son, no longer a man, a student, nor did my thoughts, my reveries of the future, have existence. All this was buried, marked by a stone on which was engraved in bold letters: HERS.

Mrs. Zucker, my mother-in-law, was addressing invitations; her husband read aloud names from a black address book, each one passing her severe censorship before it was applied to the envelope. Some were dismissed with a single gesture. Mr.

Zucker would call a name and before he could finish, the whole family would join in a whistling scream: NEHOE.

Mira stamped envelopes, licked the flaps and sealed them. An aunt was on the phone, arranging the details of the ceremony and reception. I tried to help Mira, but she scolded me. I ventured a word to the aunt on the forthcoming elections. She turned away from the phone for a moment and glared scathingly. "Oh?" I tried to catch the eye of the brother who was preparing the wine list and the food strategy, but he looked up in great bewilderment, drunk with the wine list he was studying; then, recalling who I was, he smiled feebly and resumed his business.

I smiled at a fly on the lampshade. It remained fixed in its spot, though its wings fluttered furiously. I thought: If I succeed in forgetting everything else, loving it fiercely, then I might be exalted, as in the famous Lao-tse notion which states that the essential nature of a door, though it comprises wood and hinges, is the void it encloses. What then is love? Woman? Romanticism? Lust? A lonely room?

Transcendentally, the void, the absolute—naked and devoid. This is where the fly comes in. I tried to love it with bare and abstract love, but failed to attain this grace, even as I failed to love my bride, because of the stir and bustle for which I was the reason—I, feeling myself to be the masked face of my gloomy courtyard.

Most irritating of all were the infinite instructions imparted by Mrs. Zucker. She recited, "And my tall sister is Mrs. Myerson, the second is Mrs. Morrison, the third Mrs. Abramson, the fourth, Josephson. Above all, young man, don't be like my poor brother Nathan who mixes up their names with delight. Should you offend them, there is the matter of the wedding presents to consider. May God forgive me for thinking of this, but one does not have God living on Park Avenue, only rich relatives. Now remember, all their husbands have the same first name. Mr. Myerson is blind in one eye. When he talks to you, he seems to be looking away; this is because he was cross-eyed before he began losing his sight. The fact is, when you find him staring directly at you it is a sign he is talking to someone else. The fat one, Mrs. Morrison's husband, loves to laugh. Tell him a joke. He likes jokes that are tipsy. If he asks you how much is twenty and twenty, say fifty; and when he asks you why, tell him they changed it—it used to be forty, but they changed it. He will laugh. When his wife sees him laughing she will laugh, and when she laughs her purse laughs too. When the purse laughs, you will laugh your way to the bank. Otherwise you'll be crying, and not at the bank but in the poorhouse."

"Mother . . . always the poorhouse," Mira said and went back to kissing the envelopes, her tongue arid as a desert.

"Should Mrs. Josephson's husband talk Bible, just listen. He's intoxicated with it now, and hugs his new discovery."

I was becoming more and more confused. My face was bathed in sweat, my mouth twisted upward, my feet tapped an exotic rhythm, while my hands trembled like the willow branches on our Sukkoth holiday. I saw Mira, huddled inside an envelope, her brother rushing to paste on a stamp bearing a radiant picture of their father—on his face a swollen smile, aunts and uncles peering through his teeth, marching at me menacingly, armed with Bibles printed in Chinese characters. Mumbling good night, I flee the maze of voices and find myself in the street, where a gentle breeze caresses the crowns of the trees and silent secret lights flicker in high windows.

I have a sudden wish to see Renna, my girl of the summer before. Her room is at peace, quiet; she keeps flowers in a vase. When I arrive I'm still trembling. Renna soothes my eyes, takes my sweaty clothes and hangs them up to dry. She serves me tea, steaming and good. A Haydn symphony is playing on the radio, filtering through to my very marrow, myrrh to my wounds. I take her in my arms, kiss her long lashes, remembering I had loved to kiss them the summer before. I tell her about Mira, the girl who is going to be my wife.

" 'My brothers have deceived me like a brook,' " Renna declaims. " 'Brook that is dry, and of a sudden waters come; faithless brook, our brother in most uncalled-for hours; brook fleeing inward and away at once; your entire self a source of strength and selfness.' "

" 'Midst your banks, O stream, I kiss the dew,' " I match her verse.

" 'Wild shrubs will give forth fragrance,' " she offers, laughing. Thus, we delve into a night of love in which the door is not the void, but hinges, wood and joinings. But Renna is woven of dreams, the capricious goddesses, and I must go home.

Plans for the wedding filled the subsequent weeks. Day followed empty night; Mira was busy, and I alone in my room.

One morning I was awakened by the sound of the alarm clock and realized, to my dismay, that it was ten thirty, and that in two hours I was to be married. I washed and shaved (twice, in honor of the day), dressed in the clothes I had bought for the wedding, and wearing the new pair of pants Mira had given me, I set out. I stepped into a taxi at the corner.

"Where to?" the driver asked, one hand already turning the meter.

"Where to?"

"Where to indeed? Here? There?" laughed the driver, "To One Hundredth Street or not to One Hundredth Street, East or West?"

"Wait a minute," I said, stupefied. "It's an odd thing, but I don't remember where I am supposed to go. The address is probably in my pocket."

"Take your time," said the driver.

I reached into my pocket and began to search, but my pants were new, and the pockets were empty of the mess my father used to refer to as my "rag museum." All I found was a maze of price tags.

"I'm supposed to be married today and I don't know where my wedding is to be."

The driver roared. "Maybe you left the address home."

I decided to go back and look; perhaps it was in my old pants.

The building, however, was locked and my key was of course in my other pants. It was a weekday and all the roomers, being students, were undoubtedly in school. Moreover, it was Thursday, and on Thursday the superintendent, who lives under the stairs, goes downtown to have his free haircut at the barber school. He wouldn't be back until four thirty.

I tried to break the lock, which had recently been changed because of my robbery. The entire door had been reinforced at the same time and for the same reason. There was no way of getting in.

I went across the street for a cup of coffee and called Mira's house but got no answer. They had all left much earlier. I could imagine the family, engrossed in a list of last-minute details, placing the champagne in ice buckets, and finally waiting for me.

It was then that I understood: they had neglected to invite me to my own wedding.

Shuddering, I tried to recall the name of one of the aunts or uncles . . . all that came to my mind was: Son, Aunt Son and Uncle Son, many Sons—

all together, a singular disaster. I confided my plight to the waitress, who smiled, thinking it marvelous that I was drunk so early in the day. I finished my coffee and began to walk, scanning my mind for a clue, praying madly for some hint.

I stopped at various houses and found them empty—my wedding was not taking place there, neither was it here. . . . I asked people on the street if they had noticed a wedding party assembled somewhere, and was told that if I was fortunate I might be invited to my funeral at the proper time. It was late. The sun, through heavy clouds, was cold to me and yellow as my soul.

I retraced my steps and found myself at home. The door was now open. Hopefully I ran up the three flights, thinking I might somehow find the address. I paid no attention to the fact that the door to my room was open and the light was on. An old white-haired man, his body wrinkled, stood naked in the middle of the room, waving his arms grotesquely. He looked at me with absolute composure, as if I were expected. I myself at first was speechless. Then all at once I shrieked at him, "What are you doing here, you madman?" and at the same time I began searching frantically for the pants I had worn the day before, stamping my fists on the desk so that my papers flew.

"What are you looking for, sir?" the old man asked calmly, continuing his bizarre motions.

"Pants, a pair of pants."

"There were some gray pants here," the man said, pointing to a chair, "but I made a rag out of them and wiped the floor. The super always leaves old pants here for that purpose."

"And where is the rag?" I asked.

"I threw it in the yard," he said, pointing to the open window. "One of the neighbors was burning the Sunday papers, so I threw the rag to her. She makes a fire in the yard every Thursday. I think the smell makes her happy."

"What are you doing here?" I asked, without expecting a response. Anyone who had endured a morning such as mine evidently had every reason to expect to find a naked old man in his room, making rags to wipe the floor out of his only other pair of pants.

"This is the third-floor bathroom, you know," the old man said.

"This is my room," I said, certainty fleeing, and I not moving to pursue it. "This is where I live, eat, sleep. This is where I first kissed the girl who is standing at the canopy and being married to me at this very moment. This room *was* the bathroom, but that has been moved to the old laundry room, near the fire escape."

"An age of anxiety," the old man sighed. "Every landlord makes three rooms out of one; so many people seeking shelter. Too much reproduction and not enough construction, that's the trouble with this world, my boy. There should be fewer marriages."

"I can promise you that," I said. "Fewer marriages indeed. . . ."

"What am I doing here?" he finally said, lowering his arms so that I realized his strange movements were a response to imaginary jets of water. He began to dress, nodding and talking all the while. "Forty years. Forty years I washed in this room. I go to visit my daughter, stay away six

months because of illness and now that I'm back
. . . Let no one underestimate the power of habit;
I never even noticed that someone was living here.
Habit. It's what ages the old, causes them to march
toward the end. They are so much in the habit of
life, they forget to do anything about it, and suddenly expire. If life were more attention and less
habit, we wouldn't die so soon." He took a bottle of
wine from his pocket, gave me a sip and continued
to talk. I noticed that it was now evening.

"It's good you're not getting married," he told me.

"Why?" I said. "Tomorrow or the next day I undoubtedly will get married. Mira's parents, of
course, won't speak to me, but still I'm sure we'll
get married."

He was irritated. "Look at me," he said, "eighty
years old. They've already felled the forest for my
old body. In my youth I wanted to write. I came to
live in this house, which in those days was occupied
by young writers. Even Morim Morum used to live
here. I was forty years old. My wife had died long
before, and my daughter was married. I did want
to write, but desire was in one place, stories in an-

other. I yearned to write them, but they were reluctant to be written. I waited for 'inspiration'; her royal highness would not come. She visited Morim Morum five times a day but wouldn't even glance at me. She would visit all my neighbors and I would hear their typewriters ticking far into the night. But I, who so craved her company, was never granted the pleasure. Did I not wish to kiss the moon? My stories, nonetheless, kept their place in heaven. Two months ago, when I was with my daughter in my home town, an idea occurred to me. If I were ten, twenty years younger I would have celebrated, reveled, rejoiced, chewed chairs. But it was too late. So with you. You did not get married today, which means tomorrow will be too late.

"I will tell you my idea—of course it's not an idea with apparent importance; its power is couched in subtlety like the philosophy in a lion's roar, the poetry in a train's lonely whistle, the lyric of the glowing sun. The idea is this: we age, grow old, the years race by, so that it seems to us that we have matured with the years. This is even partly true. Our faces fade, our limbs grow sore. But at night in our sleep we are like infants. Wrinkles vanish, aches go away, in dreams we become what we have always been—infants. . . ." The old man took a deep gulp of wine.

I laughed.

"Don't laugh, child, these matters pertain to you, and your poor wife as well. They've already felled the forest for my old body. . . . My wife cut the first tree, and Morim Morum cut the rest."

The old man grew pale. His face darkened, he seized my hand, leaned on me and began to weep. "Can you sing?" he asked. "Sing something with me. A round. You sing one voice, I'll sing the other. Perhaps my life will realize itself through the song."

He began to sing hoarsely. I tried to follow, to sing the second voice. At the end of the song he gulped down the remainder of the bottle, lay down on my bed, and began to speak, swallowing his words. He stopped suddenly in the middle of a word, without altering his tone one way or the other. I knew he was dead.

I called a doctor, who speculated that, after a recent bout of pneumonia, he had died of the chill contracted in the moment of nakedness, when he had stood before the open window to throw my gray pants into the courtyard where the neighbor was burning the Sunday papers and happily smelling the fire because it was Thursday. Had I not dealt with my pants in so improvident a manner, the old man would still be alive.

The next day, after we delivered the old man to the morgue and notified his daughter, I went to Mira. I told her everything. Her parents were enraged, the horde of uncles all but flung me through the window. Mira did not heed their wrath and laments. We were married that very day at City Hall, my superintendent and the neighbor woman serving as witnesses.

My wife came back from the room in which her mother was now dying. I took her hand and we left. In the street she placed her arm about my waist—comfort, deep, deep delight. Though she walked with such vigor, still she seemed small and winsome. At the corner I stopped and bought a lollipop.

"Would you like it, Mira?" I asked.

"Whether you give it to me or not, you're mine. That makes the candy mine too. Yes or no—either way—I say . . . yes." She grabbed the candy and sucked it with relish. "Daddy, how much do you love me?" she asked in a childlike voice, clinging to me like a baby. "From here to where? To that tree on the corner? To the sky? Maybe even to the river?" she continued, looking at me with mischief in her eyes.

We walked home, the autumn wind sweetening thoughts that set in with the silence, harsh thoughts we had no wish to think.

On the corner of One Hundred and First Street and Broadway a skinny Indian in native dress had a dancing monkey on a string. The monkey looked at me and said, "Hello, baby!"

I said to him, "Who's 'baby'?"

He said, "You."

I said, "Thanks."

He: "Not at all. Wait till you see what comes next!"

I: "What comes next?"

He: "No point in humans knowing what monkeys know. He-he-he! The monkeys knew when to stop. Humans didn't. They're monkeys who don't know when to stop."

I laughed back and gave him the lollipop stick. I said, "I hope you get back to the jungle and have an act with Indians on strings."

He smiled at me, the sad smile of an old Jew, and returned to his dance.

When we got home I washed a pot and made some tea. I told Mira about the long summer. She made me laugh. She told me what it was like to die every night.

"Imagine, I almost know what it is, then people

begin to applaud. I love the applause so much that I forget everything I've learned and begin to smile so they'll clap more. In the end I know nothing."

She lay close to me that night. "Why must we always be strangers?" she said. "I can't stand to be alone today. I can't stand to be me. Maybe I can be you, if only for a minute." I held her in my arms, I caressed her. We swam deep into ourselves drawing pearls to the surface, regarding the precious stones in our own light. Two bodies, one light. The pearls were dreams strung tightly together, yearning for each other. We yearned not for what was, but for what we had once hoped would be . . . what we had wanted, the two of us.

It had begun in a dream which promised much: a small house, perhaps on Mount Carmel, perhaps in Jerusalem, perhaps amid sycamores in the Galilee. Perhaps in none of these places. Somewhere else . . . a small house which words had made real enough to touch, to paint—doors green, inside whitewashed for the Pesach holiday. A child, sometimes a boy, sometimes a girl, all of us flying together to New York, watching the block city from the air, the miniature people, fields, animals. We would climb to a tall roof where all the streets end, point: "This is where Mummy was born, here is the park where Mummy met Daddy when she was so young. . . ." We laughed and laughed again.

We were not ashamed to laugh, loving our laughter and laughing our love. She pressed close to me and suddenly her laugh was a wild shout, fierce, female. Then she smiled, contented. At that moment the telephone rang.

"Don't answer," I whispered.

"Don't be silly," she said, still laughing. She picked up the phone. "Hello."

"Mira, Mira," the voice intoned. "Who is that laughing? I hear it. Fine time for jokes. Bastards!"

"What happened?" my wife asked, still gasping with laughter. "Who is it? Father? What is it, Father?"

"Your mother is dead," he said. "Laugh, if you like. . . ." He slammed the receiver.

"Father, Father . . ." she implored. "Father . . ."

Then she turned on me, kicking, throwing everything in sight: ashtrays, shoes, books. I tried to talk to her. It was no use. Her nose began to bleed. She was too weary to do anything but weep in a thin voice. I dressed her and we took a taxi to her father's house.

The family was already there—her brother, his wife Adele, her sister and her husband, uncles, aunts. No friends. There was an almost festive atmosphere in the room. The women in their best clothes at regular intervals dabbed their moist eyes with colorful handkerchiefs. The gentlemen spoke in whispers, the smoke of their cigars blending with the ladies' perfume. Uncle Nathan, "the prophet," was there too. "As the saying goes, 'Only fools are prophets,'" he used to quip, "and a word to the wise. . . . True, I myself am an utter fool, no one would deny that." Nor could anyone deny that Uncle Nathan's prophecies were always fulfilled.

Morris made no move to greet us. Embedded in the single armchair, he waited while we made the rounds of the family, all of whom were sitting on wooden chairs in a large circle. An unlit cigarette was poised between his fingers. I gave him a light. He puffed deeply, made a sad gesture with his hands. Mira fell to the floor, leaned her head in his lap and wept with him.

I sat down, oppressed by the wish to complain. Uncle Nathan sat near me. "They're waiting," he said. "What are they waiting for?"

"Not for the Messiah," I retorted. "What would they do with Him should He come?"

"Want to know what they're waiting for?" he asked, offering me a cigarette. "They're not waiting. The event is waiting . . . for them to come to it, to become part of its inner trappings. It's a good thing that death occurs in the Zucker family. Otherwise they would never be aware of one another."

"I'll take the television," I heard Aunt Ida saying to her husband. "It's a good set. She won't need it where she is now. And you'll measure the ring. Pure gold. After all, you did give it to her.

. . . She can't take it with her and Stanley is about to be married. One person dies, another marries." She sighed with mock resignation. "That's life."

"Already they're grabbing," Morris whispered to my wife. "As long as I'm alive they won't lay their hands on anything. In my grave I'll clutch every last shred."

Uncle Nathan and I wandered into the hall. From there we could see the other room. A nurse sat beside the dead woman, knitting a green pullover. "Green, the color of life, the color of money," Uncle Nathan remarked.

We went back into the main room. My brother-in-law joined us. He looked at me uneasily through his four eyes, two of which were set in black frames trimmed with gold.

"So . . . how is business?" he asked.

"What business?"

"School, and everything."

Nathan turned to me beaming, and winked fondly. "The soul of my good sister, may she rest in peace, is on its way to heaven. I'm sure of it. She's having her laugh now. All of our lives we urged her toward death, making no ceremony. Now that she is dead, we are all here in our absurd finery."

My brother-in-law flared defensively. "A fine time for jokes. She was a wonderful woman. I always respected her."

"Always," I said, nodding sardonically. "When she stood on the breadline in nineteen thirty-six, you wouldn't allow her daughter to visit her because you were ashamed."

He made no response, and finally turned to me and broke the silence. "I don't get you at all," he declared. "You are too strange. Do you know how you hurt Mrs. Zucker when you didn't bother to come to your own wedding? And now that the poor woman is dead you sit around exchanging wisecracks with Uncle Nathan, the madman who spends his life looking for the Messiah rather than for a job.

"Do you happen to know, my friend, how your mad prophet survives? I give him money, every month I do. Mrs. Zucker, though she barely managed to buy her own bread, gave him money. The whole family gives him money. A friend of yours from your own home town told me a thing or two about you. How, when you were eight years old you were passing a toy store, the window full of tantalizing objects: a red wooden horse, a giraffe, little trucks that could be made to move, a small electric train. What did you do? You flung a stone through the window, picked up the giraffe and began to run home. The storekeeper and the people in the street chased you, shouting, 'Thief! Stop thief! Stop!' They caught you. You looked at them in wonder and amazement. They surrounded you. 'First a toy animal, next money. Later who knows, our hearts maybe,' they said. The policeman who took you home asked why you had done it. 'Let them hide the toys,' you argued. 'If they don't want people to take them, they shouldn't be put outside.' And your parents were told about it, but only laughed. What a home you came from. You were never decent to us, and Mira working so hard to help support you. What if God forbid she gets sick, or pregnant? How do you expect to support her? With Spunoza?"

"Spinoza," I retorted. "He used to make eye-glasses. He left me a fortune. And if I'm really a matter of interest to you, I shall enlighten you. The subject—of me, that is—appeals to me today." I began speaking with avidity, all the more strange for me as I seldom say much to people. I had been trying to catch my wife's eye, but she avoided me.

"I'm a loathsome creature," I began with a flourish. "God's afterthought. . . . I have a pleasing face, but my soul is black. An insect is ugly, but its soul is white. You can tell when you crush one. What could be more hideous than a creature such as I, who finds sublime delight in squashing flies? Reason, in this matter, is reversed. It is they that fly. Yes, they do." My excitement was mounting. I restrained myself and steadied my voice.

"They fly themselves. Little things like that. No motor, no tricks, nothing. A mere fly can fly, but not I. It can go any place: the emperor's nose, the thumb of your archenemy. A small insect can sting any woman's buttocks. I have been allowed to greet a fragment of the universe in night's dark: a tree, the needle of a pine, a bird's flight. . . .

"This is the point, the idea, my friend, that consumes me as maggots do a dead body. It is for the sake of this ideal, independent and unrelated to my proper self, that my body is in this world. It may seem to you a slight idea, a childish one, but no. This idea is deep and has always been nourished by my total being, as necessary to me as oxygen.

"When I was an infant I was very sick. My parents, the doctors, everyone had given up hope. I suddenly recovered. For no medical reason. No one could understand it. I understood it. I knew more than all of them. They knew the science of medicine. I knew what I would wish to be in the future. You think that's funny, laugh if you like. . . .

"I was destined to embody an ambition—great, not in terms of its goal, but in the fact that I renounced other ways in order to fulfill the destiny which was granted me when the doctors despaired of my life. I will try to explain this thing to you. A sound person (one whose strength lies in what is within him) takes no interest in the fact that true greatness, of the sort I have always imagined and considered singular, abides with impotence. An example: I knew a great writer who wanted more than anything to write. His inability to be a Balzac, this was his genius. This is not to say that everyone who can never be Rembrandt is, as a matter of course, a great painter. But wherever there is a strong impulse to create, it will find its way, sometimes underground and untried. A wadi, after its bed has been carved in the sands of some unknown desert, becomes a path which others may follow, being carried like water between its mighty flanks. . . . Yet the faltering artists, those who try to find their way and fail, they will cast the new wadi in the sands of another unknown desert, graceless yet captivating, leading its creator to the peak of a mountain. A true road is never beautiful, but like the preying eagle—majestic, having been derived out of nothing. Like God.

"Mira, who as you know happens to be slightly simple-minded, once told me that when she is working on a role she feels like God. Even she has experienced that wondrous thrill. So that the goal is of no account: one wants to be God, another to lead armies, a third to spin tales which will shake the core of the world. My goal is modest, and you are amused by my wish to be a teacher, a scholar, a professor, whose entire capacities are comprehended only by himself.

"I have no wish to be one more mimic of God. Like a small boy in the water who looks around at the people bathing beside him and decrees: 'I am the Lord of the Universe; though they don't know it, still I am their King.' He devises great feats of statesmanship and, suddenly, is caught in a fierce and awesome flow of pleasure. Artists, writers, think themselves the ultimate creators. Though they are truly creators, this is the joke. . . . These artists are inventive, each in his way. Yet, where is the greatness in this condition? For they rank second in a shallow comedy. Humor is what rises upward, sees things in their proper place and orders them, having recognized justice in the disorder—a sense which presupposes identification: with Creation, with what is general, with what is 'created' in the passive sense.

"Here, my friend, is where the matter of the fly

becomes relevant. I too was once in chains. I looked at them, neither cursed nor cried. I laughed. I turned the chains into power, reversed the energy from below to above so that I could fly . . . high above the rest, serving no one. Unlike the misguided painter who tries to add another beautiful window to the world for the greater pleasure of his fellow men, that their souls may further delight in the marvelous order enclosed by a single frame . . . lovers of humanity, sticking out their tongues at one another. Idiots!

"I would rather be one flying insect than a hundred belly-crawling people. It is pain that makes him soar. I know. Pain is elevating. Another dimension, where there is always more. A place where freedom is.

"I need no one. I shall be my own provider, self-sufficient, content. The ideal lover, needing no object for my love. Height, a new dimension, defying time and space, defying the clock perched on its shelf, thinking that its ticking hours, its Olympian quiet, have the power to make me old.

"I will fly high—beyond time, where all clocks

break. I will live forever, mount the clouds and ride, godlike . . . like a fly."

My brother-in-law sat staring at me. What made me talk so much that day? Dreams that I had never put into words. Perhaps the funeral, the fear of death.

I left the room. Morris, my father-in-law, passed me in the hall, making no sign. He bent to smell the flowers in a vase, sighed deeply and went into the other room where his wife lay forever silent. He stroked the nurse's hair. She continued her tranquil knitting motions, as if the touch was familiar. He whispered something. She answered, without turning her head. He kissed her ear. She sighed.

I stood watching, hidden by the shadow of the door. On the table I noticed a picture of my wife when she was two years old, standing naked before the backdrop of an African jungle, clutching a stuffed tiger. Morris, after a prolonged look at the dead woman, left the room, closing the door slowly. He returned to his place in the armchair and, together with my wife, began to weep again.

Morning light made its way through the parted

blinds. I opened the window. Air rushed in as if it had been waiting. I wanted to jump toward it, but I held myself back.

During the war I had crossed a field in Jerusalem without knowing it was mined. Afterward Nahum had come to me. "Do you happen to know what you just did?" he asked. "No," I said. "You crossed a field of mines, you fool. Imagine what could have happened to you. . . ." He said only that much and turned away.

I remember feeling a chill through my body, a delicious chill, like the one that took hold of me now as I stood at the window. A single point of terror, endless in span and significance, overwhelming, conquering, taking possession . . . transforming me into a block of wood. A single blow with the force of a thousand; only one . . . no more.

There was another time, the battle in Bet-Eshet. I remember seeing Amos, my friend, my best friend, in the old Arab house, his eyes glowing. Gashed skin, hair falling in his face, sweating, he stood there emitting violent shrieks. The rest of the company, within eye range of the house, continued to go about their business: one soldier leaning idly on his rifle; another setting up a sack of TNT; someone staring through the window, a study in self-involvement—a scarecrow, perhaps the statue of an unknown soldier. I saw two scenes simultaneously, related only in terms of mutual indifference: shouts and cursing within the hut, quiet unconcern without.

I dashed inside; the others followed in pursuit. I could not understand the tremor, the excitement I was experiencing. The others stood in the four corners of the room, expectant. . . . They had come, pressing an outcome. The event would have sequence now, I thought. As long as they had stood outside, the consequence of this matter, whatever it was, remained suspended, waiting for the throbbing of watches to appoint a proper place.

A man's body lay on the floor, lifeless. A woman, about forty years of age, bloodstained, weeping, knelt over the body. A withered Arab woman—this one old, her gnarled face suggesting grape leaves that had been dried by the sun and cracked—stood beside her. This woman's eyes were set deep in their sockets, so that the other features, thrown into sharp relief, became circling hills. She was bewildered, and every now and then a hoarse, unintelligible sound escaped from her mouth. As I entered, Amos struck her. She sank to the ground, her fall shaking the dead man.

The younger woman, who was crouched beside the body, sobbing and mumbling softly, lunged toward Amos and spat in his face. He wiped it slowly, fixing his gaze on me. Suddenly he leaped forward, seized her, tore away her veil and stuffed it into the mouth of the old woman, who was trying to raise herself from the ground.

"Every lousy Arab woman is a soldier in the next war," he screamed. "Look, look at the shirt on him . . . on the dead man. Whose is it? Do you know? I'll tell you whose it is. It's Yuchi's. I gave him that shirt, and now that shit is wearing it and Yuchi is dead. All these goddam Arabs will be dead too. Let her house be burned—Yuchi got a bullet in his back. He's lying there, in his grave under the tree, shivering cold. They bake their bread with blood . . . Yuchi's blood."

What's there to say? I thought to myself. There is no good answer. Amos took a knife from his pack and began to stab the young woman. I wanted to stop him. Two guys who had been standing aside in silence held me back.

"What are you doing?" Rafi reproved. "He's your friend, isn't he? That's no way to act with friends."

"He needn't kill the woman," I said.

"Woman, man," Gingi retorted, "when you've got to kill, it doesn't matter whom. He's burning up inside, can't you tell? He's got to let it out, so he'll feel better. An Arab—man, woman—it's the same, the same shit." And he spat.

"Go fight on their side, you pillar of justice," Amos shouted at me. "Say poems to them." With his foot he spurned the young woman's still writh- ing form. "His father used to read him poems in the attic. He has an intellectual father . . . goes digging for antiquities and whistles Beethoven. Go ahead, join them. Raise the flag. Together you can burn the Jewish people. . . . How do you sleep nights, when you think of all the Arabs you've killed?"

"There's a difference," I tried to explain. "There's a difference." I felt a gnawing pain.

The old woman meanwhile had managed to remove the rag from her mouth. She repeated one word like a broken record: "Hero, hero, hero," and then began to cry, to scream and kiss the dead man's feet. Amos grabbed her, and with one blow she fell silent, streaming blood.

We stood there mutely before this tableau, numb with fear and crude wonder. A door we had not noticed before swung open. A boy of eight, his belly naked and bloated, a pack of flies swarming about his bald head, ran toward the old woman, flung himself into her arms and began to cry. Dust stuck in my throat like a heavy featherpillow. Amos seized the child, a mischievous glint in his eyes, and for a moment stared intently at me.

I regained my voice slowly. "For God's sake," I said. "Don't touch the boy."

"Sorry for him?" he asked, drawing his knife close to the quivering child. "Sweet kid, no? Small, fat, filthy with flies. Cute. Cuckoo-ri-koo, little sweetheart. Daani here will buy you a wooden horse on a long string. You'll walk down the street together, whistling at the cars, stopping the traffic. Right?" A flash of earnestness crossed his face. His throat muscles contracted.

"Ten years from now," he shouted, "in ten years will he still be so cute? I'll tell you how it will be in ten years. He'll quietly march himself home, pick up a rifle and sneak over to your place in the night. While you and your father sit whistling Beethoven, he'll steal up from behind and put a bullet in your back; he'll grab the first girl he finds . . . he'd screw the hole in a drawer, the bastard. Look at him, isn't he sweet!"

"Stop it!" I pleaded. "In the name of God, stop!"

"What a baby that Daani is," Gingi said with contempt.

I leaped from my corner, freeing myself from

the grip of the two soldiers who had restrained me earlier. This pair looked at Amos and then at me with identically vacant looks, as if they were twins. "I'll kill you, Amos," I said. "I'll kill anyone who comes near me." And I aimed my rifle. "Let the boy go or I'll shoot."

"You don't have the guts to kill anyone," he said, and burst into savage laughter. "I know . . ." he said caustically. "You will kill the boy. You shoot and I won't put my knife to him." He laughed again, as if illuminated by this insight.

"I'm going to shoot *you*. They are all my witnesses. I am warning you . . . for the last time." My tone was imploring.

"I give you two minutes," he said. "You shoot, or I start with the knife."

There was one shot. The child fell dead. I had fired the shot which struck him in the throat; he was dead.

Do you see? I aimed at Amos. I fired at Amos. I've always been a good shot, and the room wasn't more than three yards across. But my bullet hit the boy. Understand? I didn't shoot Amos. I tried to,

I had to! That is what I had decided. But I couldn't carry out my decision. My shot killed a little boy. He sank to the floor. The flies that had hovered about him fled to the stove in confusion and then, curiously, circled back about my head.

Stillness, along with the charred remains of bread in the oven, filled the air. I was dimly aware that the room was empty now. In the distance I heard the wild laughter of Amos. My eyes were drawn to the window carved low in the wall, framing a finely crafted landscape: a tree bent to the ground, shielding a dogshed; nearby a small well, a cluster of green cactus plants; hills on the horizon still bathed in morning vapors wafting upward, intense, merging with the sky. I poured water on the oven fire and my nerves began to steady.

My thoughts at first revolved about the window, but it seemed to send terror streaming toward me. I covered the child's body with my paratrooper's coat. I wrenched a coal from the oven and wrote on the wall, "Two children died here today."

I left the hut and went toward the rest of the unit, who were sitting idly in the shade. They were watching me. The shadow of the house, the well, the fruit groves in the distance, the leaves moist with dew and their own weariness gave their faces a new aspect. They seemed to be waiting for something. Amos too was waiting.

Amos began to taunt me, thinking, I suppose, something's got to happen . . . might as well get it over with. "Something hurt you? Don't you feel well, dear? Try throwing up." He laughed. "What are you waiting for?" He got up and pushed me. "Want to fight?" he challenged. "Fight me! You're stronger, it'll make you feel better."

"Daani is going to kill him now," Gingi called out incitingly—at the same time flourishing a picture of a naked girl, and dividing his attention between me and the picture. "He'll kill him. Just like that, he'll kill him." He repeated these words as if in a trance.

"I killed the boy," I said.

"He's got no guts," Amos countered.

"No, I've got no guts," I answered, and continued: "Two kinds of people will leave this place today, those who will remember with remorse that they did nothing to stop this from happening, and I —who tried, but failed. Nonetheless, I'll have you brought to trial. Maybe an outside law will find a way to punish you, a way to punish me too."

I watched Amos throughout this speech and sensed the meaning of this episode in his laughing eyes which, apart from the light of darting pupils taunting, slapping, riveting me to my place, were dark windows. "Amos and I cannot choose to kill each other," I said to myself, reading this message in his face. We were merely soldiers. The officer was gone. He had issued an order and gone off— the bastard—leaving no address.

What we once had been to each other, what I had once been, remained a small monument in a radish garden on the forgotten street of our childhood. Today I had killed that garden, and the road of maturity from here on would be forgetfulness. Forgetting the grubby can we kept silkworms in, long dreams with happy endings in which we discover something, grow toward something, campfires that roasted potatoes and burned us, consuming along with ourselves Bach fugues and private stars. That

Daani died. I no longer belonged to myself. I no longer belonged to anyone. I withdrew from the warm painful world to a grayness where I rode the furious horse of ambition.

I had just been born in my private graveyard at Bet-Eshet and needed to fashion new rules to live by—rules which did not relate, as I had never related, to other people—for whom one day led straight to another and not to the little boy I had killed for no reason. I remained alone, alone and choked with tears.

I stand before the window, which offers me its open view. My mother-in-law is dead in the other room. Fear stalks within. I am about to take leave of myself. I set my feet for the fall but do not jump. I sense the air's embrace. At the same time I am aware of deception in its promise of release and support. My little finger races downward and I am

drawn after—(a shattering impact). Sweet pain,
delight, agony. I break out in a cold sweat. Before
the window stands Daani waiting for Mira his wife,
who does not come. A sad story.

"Mira," I whisper. The window answers, "Don't
you understand? It's all over." "What's all over?" I
ask. No answer.

The feeling that I was among strangers had per-
vaded the room all evening. It was this feeling
which had impelled the odd monologue with my
brother-in-law. Something had happened. What, I
did not know.

Mira remained silent. I put my arms around her
and tried to kiss her. She was cold. I let her go,
feeling like a fool. Two strangers, we walked together through the morning chill, the play of wind
and trees, the game of the yellow leaves on the sidewalk. I thought to myself: fish are swimming in the
Kinneret. Great things are transpiring, wars being
fought, people coming to birth and dying. . . . It
is possible that the light we see came from a long-
dead star. . . .

"What is it, Mira?" I asked my wife in a gentle whisper.

"Nothing."

"But I know something is wrong."

"My mother is dead," she replied dryly.

She spent the night on the couch, a convertible sofa we had acquired on credit. I slept alone in the large bed, feeling like a bachelor. I dreamed a mosquito was flying up my nostrils, saying, "You will never get to the places I can get to." In the dream I opened a water faucet, but no water flowed. And we were alone. I asked my mother, "Why do I always wish I were taller than the rest?" She answered, and suddenly the water began to gush, drowning out her words.

I was back in time, in this dreamy tissue of reality where one is found when he isn't anywhere else. A song sung by Lila Murad was running through my dream. Like Murad—the Arabs' leading songbird, said to have been born in Tiberias, the town with two graves for that famous rabbi, one built by the Sephardic community, the other by the Ashkenazim, suggesting the tradition that each worldly city has its counterpart in heaven; every section of the sky is refracted in a mirror strip in man's soul, and in each man's soul this is hidden by a cloud.

I found myself in a shaded spot. A clear day was dawning, the fresh smell of leaves drenched with coffee in the panic of escape; rocks rustling faintly with the scurry of small lizards. From an orange grove in the distance the sound of well pumps . . . tick, tick, tick . . . hollow, monotonous, recalling memories. Here and there explosions. They were demolishing the houses. I heard a voice clowning; I laughed.

I laughed a laugh which froze on my face when confronted by the open sky, a broad blue mass of dancing clouds, which always seemed to sneak into view when there was a thorn in my back as I lay outstretched, as if to hurt me. The insects racing about, snug in their grassy homes, but nonetheless stuck on this stinking hill, in this war, like me, could be tolerated.

The sky—splendid, towering—extended afar, to

the sea and beyond, to so many lands, seen at this moment through ships' portholes and from placid houses where there is no war, over hearty breakfasts on open porches. Earth can be enclosed but never the sky, I thought, watching a bird that looked back at me and then went its way.

I wished I could rise up, climb to the birds, become a part of the sky, with the ability not only to go anywhere, but also to remain still. I myself was tied to a single shaded spot, and could be only there, like the trees I used to see as a child when my mother took me to the YMCA building in Jerusalem.

"The air is more solid than the ground," she used to tell me. "It can't be distorted or enclosed. Below, houses are held sadly in place. They can't fly, nor can they climb. The sky up there, when it gets tired, can simply move on, coming and going, back and forth, here and there."

Sky, unable not to be there, like us, in the war . . . yet, at the same time, outside of it.

In the afternoon my wife woke me. We returned to the home of my in-laws. There were cars at the door, some of them hired—the elegant conveyances people indulge in only once, for a funeral—others belonging to the family. We set out on the journey at the head of a long caravan.

I fell asleep and dreamed of Morris, my father-in-law, with a stump in place of his right hand, playing a violin. I woke up in terror. Outside, beyond the car window, trees were red with the beginnings of fall. Yellow leaves were strewn, here in piles, there a saffron spread, a lush carpet of self-mutilating beauty that would have liked to cry out my joy . . . instead, quiet and sadness. The skies were clear, the atmosphere pure. A delicate day, as if the world were looking in a glass through which it saw a pool of quiet waters from an old French drawing. A crisp, sour smell filled the heart with undefined longing, and something sharp and undefined was yearning through the air.

Sarah Zucker, my mother-in-law, was making her final journey. I tried to imagine myself without physical existence, but couldn't even think of myself as I had once been—a baby, a child. I couldn't imagine the world without me. Was it possible that Marco Polo at one time walked the earth, that there were once knights, lords, princes? I couldn't grasp my own memory, I couldn't see myself as I was. I remained an enigma to myself; all things were mystery. The world, traveling toward death, disembodied, laughed through a coffin.

One day the sun will freeze, hell . . . and all will be gone. I felt a tremor of fear. What if I should learn something new? Could I keep it from the world? Could I guard it from myself?

Again fear as I recalled Moshe from Workers' Housing A back home, the one-handed man who had refused to sell me a kite when I was a boy. "You'll fly it," he had said. "Next thing you'll want to fly yourself. You'll leave us and go out into the world . . . big cities, broads, everything. We will have lost our darlingest boy."

I began to whistle. My wife looked at me with contempt. At my side sat Steven Scott, tall, well dressed, agitated. He clutched his fiddle and looked wearily at the fleeting countryside. I studied him, thinking: that's his road, it belongs to him—the road to the cemetery and back. If I were alone in the world, I would stay there today. I would sit in the cemetery and wait for my turn. Steven Scott will go back, as if the point of the funeral were to have him play, as if Mrs. Zucker, my mother-in-law, had closed her eyes forever for his sake, without meaning us all to come here and learn where our roots are buried.

He stood before the gaping grave, his coat billowing in the wind, strands of hair blown back and forth, racing each other for a resting place. "His hair is having a wild time," Aunt Rachel whispered to her husband. "Artists' hair is always wild. They're wild, and that's that," she added.

He played the Andante from Bach's Second Violin Concerto. We all stood by, our hearts pinched with questions: Who will miss us when we die? What is starting there for Mrs. Zucker now, though nothing here is over?

I looked at the sky and saw a bird flying two ways at once. Into the future, into the distance. My heart followed, in two directions: to the region of laughter, to the region of envy.

Morris Zucker, my father-in-law, dressed in his usual showy style, stood in his place, breathing with heavy emotion. Suddenly, overcome by sorrow, his brows knitted together and spit trickled from the corners of his mouth. He let out a piercing shriek and wailed in a loud voice, "I want to die with her, I want us to be buried together in her grave." The attendants looked at him perplexed.

"Let me die with her," he implored. "It won't be life without her. I'm jumping." He stood alone. No move was made to hold him back. The family stared, impotent.

I rushed to him, dragged him from the open grave. Secure in the strength of my restraining hand, he made a feeble forward lurch, as if he really meant to jump. I repeated firmly, "We won't let you." The family looked at me with gratitude. They seemed to be saying, "You played your part well."

Uncle Nathan, the prophet, winked at me furtively. I didn't acknowledge him, although I usually enjoyed this sort of exchange. Morris Zucker began to cry again. "Sarah, my good Sarah." He walked behind me toward the cars, sobbing and leaning on my wife. I watched him.

Once we were in the car, the red trees began to glide by. How odd, I thought, a man inviting a musician to play at his wife's funeral while she is still living; it's a good thing fate made her die.

Trees never lie: in winter nude, green with promise in spring. I opened the window and stared at them. "Thank you for being here," I said. Steven Scott looked at me derisively and began to whistle through his handsome teeth. He whistled well. I was thinking of my Tiberias grandmother, whose grave is marked by a eucalyptus tree and whose memory is enshrined in a string of pine cones.

Everyone in Tiberias feared my grandmother. Her nine sons, their wives and children, their friends—all who entered her house quaked before her. She used to give an eyewitness account of the defeat of Napoleon's fleet in the Acre harbor. She related Bible tales in the first person: "We had a Jew in Hebron, Abraham, to whom God said one day, 'Take thy son, thine only son, whom thou lovest . . .'" etc. I was her one friend. I will tell you how this came about.

I used to love to swim in the Kinneret early in the morning. I was six years old and was considered a clever child, although I hadn't spoken a word until the age of three. My cousin Reena talked, but I did not. Yehoshua Meyerowitz shouted, "Mama, Mama, boy, horse." I remained silent. Yossi, who later became a speculator, said, "Sweet-smelling flower." I was mute, unyieldingly mute. My mother dragged me from doctor to doctor, but there was no help.

One evening in Tiberias at my grandmother's house I went up to the roof with my father. He used to read Goethe by the light of a small oil lamp, the gentle breeze of the Kinneret enhancing the evening's pleasure. The half-moon was like a question mark set in the sky, so I turned to him and said in a clear voice, with perfect poise, "Father, the moon is broken. Get a ladder so we can climb up and fix it."

My father all but devoured the oil lamp in his great confusion and ran in a state close to shock to report to my mother. She in turn ran to my uncles, my uncles to my grandmother, who gave the event a logical explanation: "He had nothing to say, so he didn't say it. . . . He'll make up for it now—and one day they'll have to build a dam to shut him up." Still, she ran to relay the news to the neighbors.

It was assumed, from that day, that I would become a poet. I recited poems long as the exile of Israel and equally doleful. My mother, who is by nature a worrier (to this day she worries where the stars fall to at night, and what happened to the ten lost tribes), expressed her concern by providing me with an endless number of lyric gems to memorize and deliver—for my own good, of course. So overwhelmed was I by this kindness that I ran away from my mother to the lake one morning, and could hear her voice trailing after me. "Why did he run away, why? Doesn't he know it's for him that I do this! One day he will grow up and be grateful. I know best what's good for him."

I took off my clothes and gave my body to the water. I floated, so alone in the morning hush . . . seaweed. I watched the sun above as the waters below tickled my back. In a loud voice I said: "Sun. Daani's nice sun. My own sun. My sun-un-sun-un-un. . . ." I sang a song hardly appropriate for a poet of my rank:

Hayim Bilbayim
went to Yerushalayim
and fetched a pail of water. . . .

Hayim Bilbayim
went to Yerushalayim
and drank water in joy from the wells of
*   salvation. . . .*

Suddenly I saw my grandmother, bare from head to toe, bathing not a yard away from me. What struck me first was the simple, almost tangible contentment in her smile. I stood marveling at this. She saw me and turned pale.

At first she was fixed to the spot. Then she dashed, as if stung by a serpent, to seek shelter among the reeds on the shore, still stunned. Her face was livid.

I knew I had done something wrong, but I did not know what. Someone was opening a window to me and saying, "Here is the secret." Inside there was a vase with flowers. I clutched the vase. I sensed danger, and like Balaam's ass, I began to spew words, praising, extolling, glorifying her in elaborate phrases that ran into one another.

"You're so beautiful," I said. "Such very white skin. . . . I love you. I love you like the sad eye of the donkey loves its braying. If I was thirteen, if I was big, I would marry you and we would have grandchildren . . . me, my brother Yossi, and maybe a sister. You're like the daughter of Pharaoh in the Pesach story." I blushed.

She came toward me with a savage glare. This gave way to a smile, at first twitching, tentative, then unreserved. Her words were fierce, but her arms embraced me, and her face assured me that the danger had passed. I felt a glow of victory, for I had conquered the formidable woman regarded by the entire town with awe and terror. She dragged me home, scolding and petting me all the way.

The alliance between us remained a mystery to everyone. We laughed together in the evenings, swam together in the mornings, causing no end of bafflement to the entire family. She died, by her calculations, about 260 years old. One must make allowances here and there. All the same, one of her fictions was worth a hundred ordinary truths to me. A eucalyptus tree rises from her grave. I wish I could make my body a tall monument to her.

Through the window of the funeral car trees continued to flash by. Before long the tall buildings of New York closed in on the scene and childhood was gone. We were home.

Not long after, my thesis was accepted. I passed all the exams, became an instructor and began to teach. Immersed in the multitude of problems of research and teaching, I was unperturbed by the fact that what I regarded as a conquest, the effort for which I had mobilized my every talent, evoked a sneer from my contemporaries. My field was not popular, which added another level to the furtive joy it afforded me. Indeed, who was affected by the deep meaning I perceived in the myth and lore of a remote, cave-dwelling people whose contribution to our history was nothing at all, who didn't write Bibles or create philosophies or invent anything of any importance? What if I did unravel their strange language and bring to light the fact that this people counted only to three, believing that more than three was infinite? The inscriptions on the pottery, the sequence of the ruling dynasty, the tale of the great queen whose tongue was cut off and who then married herself to a dead horse in a glorious ceremony, giving rise to a glowing mythology which, as set forth by generations of poets, is essentially an immortal critique of the ruling classes. . . .

Some of my colleagues and a few students did express interest. But with or without their response I felt great delight. I taught with excitement, as if I were seeing the gypsy's crystal ball in my students' eyes. My life, which had been filled with dreams, was now assuming palpable worth. I was surrounded by students glowing with the thirst for knowledge. I would collect their papers, give absolute attention, feeling that their eyes relayed a gentle message which fanned my heart and eased my nerves.

This was not the dreamed-of unknown I had always envisioned; this was new. This crystal ball disclosed only the present. The future was transposed into *now,* no longer spans of meaning, nor high mountains; nor did I run, breathless. For I *was* high up, though not quite at the top of the mountain. The peak was near, I already breathed its fine fragrance.

Mrs. Zucker's death was gradually becoming a memory which crouched unspoken at the lowest, most secret levels of consciousness, like a dormant beast, a wild horse running madly in a sealed room —manifesting itself in my wife through signs I could not interpret. I remember that I came back from the university one day and wanted to take her in my arms. On her face was the presence I had noticed the day of her mother's death, when standing near the window I was trying to catch her eye. She seemed to be looking right through me, as if seeing my back and far beyond, which made me uncomfortable. I took her in my arms. She trembled and closed her eyes. I thought she was crying and, kissing her eyes, my lips became moist and salty.

I said to her, "Your tears are salty."

She laughed viciously.

I asked, "Why are you laughing at me, Mira?"

She said, "What a funny man you are, holding me in your arms, yet I am not held. Nor will I ever be held again. No man will touch me."

I asked her why. She wouldn't answer, only repeated, pensively, "No man will ever touch me. . . ."

She slipped out of my arms, sat in a chair across

from me and began to speak.

"Daan, I love you, with all my heart and soul—I don't care if you beat me, scream at me, ignore me. . . . You can teach Afghanistan poetry in a school for the deaf and dumb if you like . . . only don't ever touch me again. Don't kiss my face, my body. I no longer have a body, because it's dead. I don't expect you to understand, how could you?

"My Uncle Nathan is waiting for the Messiah. He spends the days calculating when He will come, riding like a fool on a white donkey, blowing a trumpet. Trumpets, indeed! For my mother and me the trumpets have already sounded. My mother and I have seen the Messiah, looking like the devil's caldron. . . . Whatever you do, don't touch me, Daan."

I intended to question her, to try to discover what had happened. But there was a call from the university, and who am I to fathom a dog's whine, a woman's cry or even her thoughts, which are governed by their own particular logic?

In this manner many days passed. I arranged my papers, put in order the notes that had accumulated in the course of the years, erected tidy piles on my desk which I contemplated with great emotion and which till then had looked like the nightmare of a German soldier. At the university, people were beginning to wonder why so many students attended my lectures; perhaps it was my fervor which animated the dry material. Or, on the other hand, it could have been the very remoteness of my subject from matters of everyday life, making it a separate world with distinct rules and methods. I could account for my success no better than anyone else.

I enjoyed the respect of the students, their awe when I disclosed a new theory, deciphered another inscription, expressed an illuminating idea. I loved to see their eyes shining and to hear their quiet ecstasy. I was like the man who is so secure in his wisdom that he does not hesitate to appear a fool. I gave not a thought to the churning world which, undoubtedly, considered me to be the reverse of its concept of success: a wistful clown, tedious and devoid of wit.

My wife used to watch me, dizzy from my madness. Again, she joined various road companies and was gone a lot of the time. Except for Uncle Nathan, the prophet, I had no visitors. He would come, put a pot full of water on the stove, wait for it to boil. Then he would scour a large teakettle, take a glass from the cupboard, drape a towel around his neck and begin to gulp down tea, holding a lump of sugar between his lips; from time to time, he would emit a deep sigh.

He would ask me about my papers and I would tell him.

"Interesting," he would say. "Like Sherlock Holmes. First one clue, then another, before long you've got a new language that's been forgotten for a thousand years. When I look at that pottery I can barely tell what it is; you look at it and see the past before your eyes as if there were no bounds to time, as if it were a single mass split into small units. May I read your big paper?"

"Why not?" I said. "I hope you enjoy reading it as much as I enjoyed writing it."

Uncle Nathan read it, and did not stop at that. I, being so busy with my work, did not consider showing it to the university press, but he took it and gave it to them. They read my work and were introduced to the black cave tribes, their strange culture, the legends and folklore I had collected, the stone that had been hidden in water for centuries—one face of it covered with an inscription in this people's script, on the reverse face a parallel inscription in a more familiar script, most of which had already been deciphered. By studying both sides of this stone from photographs I gathered, I was able to add to what was known of the more familiar language and, at the same time, rediscover a hitherto extinct tongue.

My work was received with enthusiasm. The university press was determined to publish my paper and I, seeing that they were anxious, was certainly not unwilling. On the contrary, I co-operated as well as I could, expending much time, tension and emotion on the proofs. I was busy with my work and knew of nothing else.

One day Mira came home. She came up to me and said, "Hello."

I mumbled, "Hello."

She said, "Did you pay the rent?"

"No," I said. "Wasn't it paid, just a day or two ago?"

"A day or two . . ." she shrieked. "I've been gone two months and you never noticed," she added sadly.

"I was busy, Mira," I told her, and explained that my paper was about to be published.

She didn't answer, only looked at me, her eyes sad, and said, "You are crueler than any serpent. . . . You, you mad professor! A heartless man, a stranger, an evil stranger to me and to the world. I hate you because you are so cold, because nothing moves you, because on your own wedding day you didn't bother to show up."

Mira was pale. Her face was flaming whiteness. She was screaming in such a way that her words swallowed each other. Her hands trembled. I sat down in shock—what had moved her to such a sudden outburst?

"You're always racing, with your crazy idea, your ambition. I've never seen anyone like you. You're afraid of high places, try to seize your own shadow, lovingly embrace the fear of death and

height. I hate you because you killed my mother!"
This was said with a shriek that sent tremors
through my body. She began to cry hysterically
and ran out of the room.

Again she's spinning riddles, I thought. She
doesn't want me to love her and stays with me for
that reason. She claims that she loves me. How is it
that I didn't notice she'd been gone for so long? My
most secret dreams are at last assuming flesh, being
realized! And now she says I killed her mother.

I called Mr. Zucker and asked him to have a
talk with her. "Mira blames me for Mrs. Zucker's
death. . . ."

He laughed. He sensed trouble and was happy,
being a man who is nourished by other people's
troubles. He would have something to talk to his
brothers and sisters about: "There's trouble between Daan and Mira." Such sweet trouble. . . .
He would have liked to lap it up, like a child with a
cupcake.

My wife came into the room and found me talking to her father. She heard his laugh, and began to
berate him too. "What are you laughing at? You're

no better than he is . . . making love to Mother's nurse on her death bed! Don't tell me fairy tales. Every day, in all the years of your marriage, you were unfaithful. And with whom? With two-bit whores. . . . You ought to be ashamed. Daan buried her, but it was you who killed her."

Mr. Zucker began to weep. Mira wept. The two of them wept and begged forgiveness of each other. They vowed mutual devotion, and that Good Mother Zucker would always be remembered. They recounted many sins, indulged in breast beating, revealed their darkest confidences, recalling bygone days when the mother was still alive and I was far away. They cried.

I would spend the days now reading galleys, which would return to the printer and reappear as final proofs, my ecstatic soul springing forth to greet them. In the evening I would go out for a walk.

Before me was New York. This giant metropolis, a single mass of strength concealed in secret arteries, a riddle to natives and visitors alike; all the more so to me, having come from such a distance, from a place where the good sun is benevolent, where desert breezes rend one's senses, where small houses make towns and where trees overshadow rooftops, where one feels the pulse of a great revival—every home having been built yesterday, everywhere a city projected for tomorrow. Here, what is seems to have always been, from the time of the Indians, as if it were they who made the high buildings, dug the tunnels so the subways would dart underground, even under ships in the river.

All was well with me and with New York, the city which swallowed me. We made no demands of each other, except that I, for my part, used the litter baskets and waited for the green light when crossing the street. No stringent demands, compared to those in my country where people are "pioneers." Here one can drift through the streets, devour fairy sights, see warm lights go on in high places, each one implying mystery; watch windows opening, hear the secret of a million people rustling in a roaring silence. I would return, quiescent, to my room, soothed by the knowledge that all are together on this lone island in the Atlantic, between the two great continents, Brooklyn and the Bronx. The throbbing city, indifferent to my isolation, my self-involvement, grants me the right to be lonely. Here we reconstruct no universe, nor do we fashion history. I am merely myself and whatever I wish to become. I loved New York for being a city that welcomes strangers. I, being foreign in every sense, in my childhood, in dreams, my land, in war and in the underground—I, who have always been a stranger, had found a home that welcomed me.

Nathan, the prophet, believed in his own instinct, or more accurately in what he termed "the marvelous intuition of fools," whose wisdom lies in what they do not know, in what they fabricate, in their great innocence, akin to cunning, rooted in that true wisdom which needs no guide, unlike what is commonly called wise; which resides in the depths of a heart, recognizes that all is granted by God, apart from awe of Him. Upon this instinct Uncle Nathan based his conviction that I, like him, was a prophet, albeit in reverse. He looked ahead, believing that the future already exists, as a painting does, and waits to be drawn up from the wells of consciousness. Maintaining that we two were brothers: I, who saw backwards, revealing an unknown sequence of dynasties, and he, who proclaimed what would come, foretelling that the cold war would be resolved on a high mountain in Albania, where a great conflagration would consume all but one tree and a single cat that would wail into the snow and be buried in it.

Uncle Nathan told various people about me; they told others, who passed on the word to some journalist, and he to another, until one wrote an article about me: a mere youth, odd, withdrawn, alone in New York, pursuing clues in books, tracking these down in archives of antiquities, finding support and authorities, evolving a theory about a people no one had heard of, proving its existence, recovering its literature, its folklore, the history of its ruling dynasty, the legend of the queen, etc. My discovery coincided with the publication of my book, and my name soared on the wings of this concurrence. I was thrilled by the publicity. I loved to be talked about. People who had read my name in the paper lowered their voices a tone when addressing me, tried to play up to me with wit. I was pleased and reverted to childhood dreams, to childhood itself.

My mother used to tell me, "Daani, you hate bitterly, yet you don't know how to spit. You were always jealous of other children, who were much more cruel than you. You always tore your new pants on purpose, so I would have to mend them. . . . You were too young to go to war. The others were older than you. Having always hated any act of cruelty, you could not find your place in war as others did. Yet you went."

When I was a child my mother used to take me to the seashore, and from there the four-story buildings looked yearning and proud. She would point to them and say, "When you grow up, you will live up there. You'll live high, so you can always watch the sea stretching beyond you; your heart will be purged by that fierce beauty. You want to go to war because others go; you want to curse because others are crude. You will be far from everyone else, and in this way close to yourself. . . ."

Mira seemed to be changing. She always had a gift for relating unconnected events: if she called a friend and got no answer, then called someone else with the same result, she would immediately conclude that the two were together, at some party from which she was being deliberately excluded. It was this means of perception which postulated the link between me and her mother, between me and the fate of the Zucker family, between our love and the course of the stars, between my name and any particular stroke of fortune. I learned that she kept a doll, called by my name, which she would prick with pins in order to cause me pain. Her thoughts were fixed on her mother; in every phrase she uttered was her mother's name. Whenever the phone rang she would shriek: death, death, death. I decided to laugh at her, thinking to myself: She has played death in so many "modern" productions, she has become enamored of the concept, and is finally possessed by it.

The truce with her father thrived on all this. He came to our house every day; they used to talk about Mrs. Zucker. When he tired of this he would go home and watch mystery stories on television, then call his relatives to inquire what new calamities had befallen them.

Truly wondrous things were occurring in my life. My fame was assuming such dimensions that there was talk of making a film of the queen's life. I had no time for my wife and her madness. One day, when I had been gone from the apartment for a while, I returned to find her waiting for me.

She said, "I have to talk to you."

I said, "I'm busy, we'll talk later."

"No," she said, and her voice jerked, holding back tears.

"I can't," I insisted.

That night she left me. She was ironing a blouse, for a while silently, absorbed in her work and her thoughts. Then she took a chair, placed it opposite me and sat staring directly into my eyes. Finally she said, "You killed my mother."

I was infuriated by her courage, the ability to fix an unshifting gaze on me, to resist confusion when my eyes met hers, to persist.

"All my life I loved my mother," she said. "Suddenly you came. She didn't want you. She thought I had found myself a madman. I fell in love with you without realizing that you have a stone in place of a heart, that you have never felt love. My mother knew this, and that's why she hated you. She loved me . . . because of my broken heart, she hated you. At her deathbed you stood without understanding why she never said your name. But I understood. A mother's love is something that's taken for granted. . . . I lived with you, for pleasure—loving you gave me pleasure. But decadence lurks in your eyes, looks out on the world according to the terms of some private armistice."

Her voice and her gaze pressed on. "My mother was far away. A thin halo was cast over my soul. In this dream my mother's presence was like the smell of freshly baked bread, fragrant, enticing. I woke to find you—a stone wall against which my head was pounded, shattered and shattered again, but never broken. You brought a big wind that carried away the good smell, and I looked at you lying beside me, so absolute, stroked your hair and said: How handsome you are! You smiled indulgently as if it didn't make you happy to hear such cozy talk. And I used to cry.

"Why is there so much crying with love? It was wrong to love you. I was the only one in the world who could. Yet, when you want to, you can make anyone fall. You have a knob you like to twist, as if it were a charm that makes you clever, dashing, loved. Then suddenly you wrench it sharply back and pounce with some vain phrase, to show that nothing moves you, that you are perhaps the only person I have ever known who needs no love.

"I gave you money. You stayed home and studied, as if it was owed to you, believing the world exists so Daani can get his degree . . . ambition leading you in the end to a point where you and only you can know its fruits.

"To be a woman—to know ultimate woman pleasure—this was as difficult for me as for my mother. We were oppressed, each of us, by a heavy burden. Full of energy and passion for life, we would race on, until some inner gate held back the pleasure, declaring: This far; from here on, suffer.

"I never told you this. That night, when my father called, remember how we laughed? That was my first time . . . for years, nothing had happened. My mother died—a devil came and released the brake. . . . It was a spell you cast that brought the devil to kill my mother.

"You won't understand any of this, just as you couldn't understand how the gypsy knew so much. There are links outside of us, beyond, which you know nothing about. You killed her, and your seed that flowed through my body calls out from her grave."

I looked at her, realizing that the girl I had found some years ago had turned into a woman. If I could deceive her now, make her believe I was hurt, she might forgive me. But I could not.

A voice whispered, "Pay no attention. Like all women, she lies. Soar . . . up . . . up . . . up. . . . Remember the fly." Other thoughts intruded. Why was I not hurt? And something else, a feeling of debt. A sense of duty, or so it seemed to me. Or perhaps a generous instinct flashing suddenly, from the place where all answers lie, this being the greatest wonder, that there is a place which holds the answer. Even the answers that have no questions . . . what a mother is to a child.

More than a sense of debt, there was a drive to win, not to allow Mira to make the final move: "You have to wait for Daan to grant you leave. . . ." I told her what had happened in the Arab village when I killed the boy who wore flies on his head. My narrative glowed with color, reached to the roots of my soul, dredging them up as if I wanted her to trample them with her frenzied dances, to find joy in my misfortune, my impotence, my inability to carry out any task that I set for myself, our marriage.

Now I no longer think it was generosity, nor was it a sense of debt which impelled me to tell my war story. In fact, it was the absolute reverse. I wanted to convey to her that everyone has his "before," during which time he raised silkworms, dreamed of a never-never land under his own town, suffered unrequited love, was ecstatic over a violin concerto, thrived on his mother's milk—but that suddenly something happens, and this event affords the chance to choose. Obliged to pass through fire one runs toward it, either scattering the fire, or being seared by it. It requires great strength to singe the fire. . . .

There was a quizzical element in my words. My entire argument appeared to be a display of unspeakable egotism and self-esteem; yet I was never prone to pride. I had always been modest, my entire effort being without pride. I had never sought to be a chief among lions; my quest was for simple greatness, to be the most handsome in a shelter for the blind.

I told her, "Without pride, Mira. I know that what was lost forever in that stinking village was the chance, someday, somewhere, to act with pride. Some months later, I took the case to a regiment court. Actually, I tried to make light of the entire episode. But Amos pressed me, and the teasing of our unit forced the issue.

"The trial took place on the lawn beside the mess hall. The entire division lingered indifferently to hear the verdict, although everyone knew what it was likely to be. Odd proceedings, formulated at arbitrary moments and made into ritual with incidental content, later elevated and sanctified. Finally the pendulum swings all the way and ritual loses sight of its own purpose. This, I thought to myself, observing the huge machinery which I had involuntarily set in motion and whose existence I was expected to justify, is why churches have form, though God is formless. I had to assume a positive role, although my position was in essence negative. I had come forth to expose forgotten wounds, to recite the names on mossy tombstones.

"I was asked a few humiliating questions. 'You know we are at war? That Arabs are treacherous fiends? That they started a war we didn't seek? That we are trying to build a home for the remnants of six million Jews killed in Europe, because not one country in the world was willing to open its gates to them while still alive or after being made into soap? That these vile Arab monsters, camped in filth, in malaria-infested swamps, would rape your mother—and that they're no good? That they . . . they . . . they. . . .'

"Amos rose to the witness stand (a table in the shade of the mess hall), and told a story. It was his defense. How there was once a settlement in the south. How everyone there was for brotherhood and making peace with the Arab neighbors. How there was one man there, Gamil, a sly Arab bastard, fat, ugly and crippled. He sold watermelons for three *grush* a head at a time when watermelons were worth one *grush* in the market. But he was an Arab, these virtuous people reasoned, and so he would be the first one with whom they would establish equal brotherly relations.

"They bought his rotten watermelons at his inflated price, invited him to their homes, gave him their daughters to dance with at their celebrations, denied him nothing. Their eyes would fill with warm compassion at the mention of this noble Arab's name. Let no one be caught haggling with him because of his lower status . . . let it not occur to anyone that it is possible to ride into town and buy watermelons there for only one *grush*.

"When the riots began, the Arabs attacked this settlement in the dead of night. It was Gamil the Good, the Righteous, who knew the inner roads of the settlement, who led the attackers. Gross, deformed, ugly Gamil led his fellow Arabs to the girls' rooms, played a leading role in the violence there, went off smiling to start a fire in the silo, a fire that spread through the entire settlement.

"Everyone laughed at Amos' story. The commander, who was judge, also laughed. The politico, who was the second judge, laughed. I was not called to the stand. At my request that I be penalized, the laughter mounted to a pitch. I heard myself being called Gamil. After a while I too began to laugh. It's hard to stand apart at such a time. I wished I could spit crudely like the rest. I wished I could be like them."

My wife spoke, sitting deep in the easy chair: "If all this had really happened to you . . . you would wake up to its meaning and recognize the evil of what you did. This would turn you into someone else."

Outside was a driving downpour. I wanted to be close to her, to forget the story, to forget everything. But she seemed to cling to the chair and its shadow. The melancholy sound of the rain seeped inward, and there was no way of chasing it.

"You can go," I said.

She said, "We will never be able to make love again. You want to live without people because you killed a small boy—and because of your wild ambition. I walk in the garden because I love to smell the flowers. I see a nice one . . . I pick it. A ray of sunlight comes my way . . . I look at it. A butterfly . . . I chase it. If a man has a mission, as you claim he does, then the flowers and the sunlight ought to recognize it, and every splinter is a butterfly; it's more rightly their secret, the secret of the entire garden, than mine.

"That's why I'm going. The world draws me. I am content to live here, with the butterfly, the ray of sun, the smell of flowers. But you hate: people, the sweat smell of love, all that makes man human. You've failed in smaller things, and in much more important ones too, than in your story.

"We will never be able to love," she repeated weepily. "With a single kiss you killed my mother and shattered me."

I never saw her again. She wrote to me, asking me to have her back. I knew this was only because it was hard for her to be alone. When I received her letter I cried. I have cried three times in my life. Once, when I saw Nahun drown in the pool in the Hadassah Park. Another time, when I was twelve. I was standing on the roof of our house, gazing at the sky and enjoying my private star. Yehoshua came up to play with me.

"What are you looking at?" he asked.

"The sky."

"Why?"

"I have my own star up there," I answered with a wink.

"I have one too," he said shyly. "Let's unite them," he volunteered, "into one big state."

"Okay. You show me yours, and I'll show you mine." He raised his hand and pointed upward.

"See the big one there? At the end of the Great Bear? Count forty-two to the left."

I started counting, thirty . . . thirty-nine. . . . My heart began to pound. Forty . . . forty-one

. . . forty-y-y. . . . "It couldn't be," I shrieked.
"That's *my* star."

"No it isn't," he insisted. "It's mine."

"There are millions of stars in the sky. I chose
such a little one . . . not the most brilliant, or the
most spectacular. It's not mentioned in books, or in
Zakai's column in the paper. No one ever paid any
attention to it. Now you come and steal it away
from me." I cried and cried.

The third time was the day I got my wife's letter. I was watching television when it came. Bette
Davis had just swept down the winding staircase
and discovered that her husband had returned
. . . blind. She need no longer mask her old age;
he would always see her as the beauty he had left
behind many years ago. I suddenly remembered the
letter and cried—or you might say that I cried and
my tears recalled the letter.

I didn't mind the loneliness after she was gone. I
am the sort of person who enjoys bad weather. It
arouses longings in me which I can explain in terms
of nature. There is no such thing as sadness—for

only it brings joy, rescues me from sadness . . . just as there is no law that protects you from the law.

I was working with demonic fervor. I had no friends. In my years in New York I had managed to offend almost all my acquaintances. I had driven some of them from my home. It was my wife who used to invite someone to dinner every now and then. They stopped coming and our fine china was never used. Now that I was alone, the house was piled high with dirt. The thick carpet was littered with crushed cigarette butts and rotting orange peel. In the evenings I used to go for a walk, stop in at the bar across the street, have a shot and go back to my work.

I loved to ride out to the airport, to trace the planes as they took off and landed. I used to stand on the deck near the field and follow the expanding speck as it approached, circling, slanting its wings downward, piercing the atmosphere with its great noise again and again; finally sinking quietly, motors hushed, body still, one last circle—and from nowhere the scurrying of signal flags, flickering lights, shouts, echoes, moving ladders. The doors open. People veiled in sleep, smiling recognition and gratitude for the stability of the ground and the freshness of the field, careless as it seemed, yet providing every comfort: a restaurant in the middle of the world; stewardesses, chic, smiling, carrying trim suitcases. After a few hours of intimacy with this marvelous commotion, I would return home to solitude and quiet.

One night on my way back from the airport I stopped the bus at the cemetery and got off. I remembered Mrs. Zucker, my mother-in-law, and decided to visit her. The place was deserted. I got the idea of taking flowers from one of the elegant graves and putting them near Mrs. Zucker. My wife used to tell me how she loved flowers more than anything . . . oceans of flowers, blossoming oceans, fragrant and colorful.

"Take them," I said. "Take these flowers and enjoy your eternal rest. Even in that infinite sleep the fragrance will be good. How many times in your sixty years on earth could you enjoy this sweet smell? All your life it was what you really wanted.

Instead you bought waxes and brushes, gadgets for the kitchen, brooms, new shoes for the children, a chair for your husband—and what was left? There was nothing left for flowers.

"Only the lucky ones, the ones who—after all the soaps, dresses and brooms—still buy flowers, they can breathe deeply, smile to themselves and say: this is it. Or the ones who buy only flowers and say: to hell with the rest!"

I began to visit Mrs. Zucker regularly. I would stop at the cemetery, go to her grave, attend to the flowers and have long talks with her. The quiet there, the peace gave me strength. Nature's beauty was an answer to the clamor in my head.

There are more birds, more trees, more open sky, more freshness in a New York cemetery than in any other part of this great citadel-city. We used to sit together, Mrs. Zucker, my dead mother-in-law, and I, and smell the flowers from the two tropics of time. We were united by the death smell from which each delivers himself. I was reminded that even in war, amid webs of death, in the foxholes, flowers smell sweet.

I began to notice the women who came to mourn their dead. One day I got into conversation with a young girl who was placing flowers on her husband's grave. She was blonde. Her face looked so lively beside the small gray grave she was tending. We left together, ate, went to see a Danny Kaye movie and laughed. Then we went to her place. This same sequence was repeated. A second time. And a third.

I have never chased girls. Since childhood it seemed to me that this was a breach of good taste. But here in the shade of gravestones I became a strip of life in a dead field, like a gay boat on a hot day in the Dead Sea. I found girls ready and yearning for love. I didn't seek them out, they seemed to come here and wait for life to take hold of them. My life had actually begun at the grave of the little boy in Bet-Eshet. The cry "Gamil, Gamil," which echoed in my ears wherever beautiful women sat waiting for men to take them, was silenced here.

One day I met Sandy. She stood tall and golden-haired beside a small stone between two large ones. I went up to her and scanned the stone. It was unmarked. She hardly noticed me.

"A grave?" I asked.

"No," she answered. "Yes and no. Yes, yes." She looked at me imploringly. "Leave me alone."

I turned to go.

"No, don't go. You have kind eyes." She put out her hand and held me back.

I waited in silence.

"Why don't you ask me?" she said.

"Husband?" I asked.

"No."

"No name?"

"She didn't die," Sandy said. "She's alive."

Then she told me her name and I told her mine. She looked at me sheepishly, swept some leaves from her golden hair, and began to speak.

"She's alive. She didn't die. She'll eat ice cream in many colors: chocolate, coffee, cherry. . . . She'll suck large lollipops, grow braids that will bob across her back on the way to school. She'll laugh when her breasts begin to show; at night she'll deplore them and dance naked in long moonlight dreams. She will be a woman, complete, her entire body in womanhood, yet mute and childlike. She'll grow old, and wise, rich with tales for her grandchildren, and then she'll die.

"All those long years she will never know that here, under this small stone, I buried her when she was one month old. Do you understand?"

She laughed, a broad open laugh, and I realized that I was making a ridiculous effort to mumble an answer. She bent down and kissed my eyes gently.

"Let's get out of here," she said. We left.

It was a spring evening. The tall buildings were silhouetted on the horizon, darkening, compressed together, restless, set on fire by the setting sun.

"It's good to be alive! Good to be alive and breathing in this graveyard," Sandy said. Shifting suddenly, her face assumed a somber cast and she began to talk.

"Once upon a time there was a seaman. There was also Sandy. There was a night of beautiful love. Once . . . millions of years ago. He disappeared. Flew away. Far. Far. Period. There are

hundreds of stories like it every day. Cold statistics
. . . the world can be viewed through the loops of
the number eight.

"In this case the sequel was slightly different. I
was pregnant and had to have the baby. I knew I
couldn't afford to keep it. Also, I thought, a child
should have a father. An agency found a good family for my baby—I sold them the baby before it
was born, they kept me in the months of the pregnancy. I never met them; it is against the rules. I
was supposed to eat well, to sleep deeply, to be-
have in harmony with their child growing in my
body.

"I will never forget those days. My stomach
grew larger. I seemed to be shrinking because of
the creature within me. As if the miracle in my body
unfolded only because I myself was contracting to
give it room to grow. It seemed to strike against my
stomach, to bounce like a ball, to quake. I could
almost hear its heart beat. Only one sad guest was
present at this gay party: my dead soul. No joy, no
excitement, only deep sadness and disquiet. I was a
paper mother. A human being grew and matured

in me, and I didn't love it. I didn't glow when the life in me stirred. I wanted only for the months to pass, so that I would deliver it to the agency, be rid of it and begin to live again. I said to myself: Poor Sandy, there's nothing between you and this creature. Did you want it? Did you love its father? Can you be a mother to it? I had no desire to bring the creature into this world. But I had already had four abortions and could not have another. What was there between me and this life that continued to swell my body?

"The father was an officer on a boat, a stranger in this country. We had one drunken night together. He docked in New York, went out on the town and found me. I was alone then, and bored. I yielded to his beauty. Next thing I knew, I was bringing a new life into the world. I don't even remember his country, except that it's the same as yours. I knew it the moment I saw you. I don't remember the name of that land of yours, but I know that his name (which I've forgotten) was written backward, that is from right to left, on his neck. He had such a lovely neck, like a swan. He cried when he took me. All the time he spoke of his hardness, how he despises a man who spills his soul as if it were a pot of water. He cried while he loved me . . . there's something sweet in that, no? You are from that country . . . no?"

"Yes," I told her. "But how did you know?"

"You both have the same expression on your faces, a sort of childish mischief concluding in earnestness, which dwells absurdly in the ridges of the mouth where all secrets are concealed. But this is only a speck of what is buried deep in a particular moment. I look and suddenly know. One day, I met a man in the street—a sad Jew. He began to talk to me. I said to him, 'You're waiting for the Messiah. You foresee the future.' He began to cry, as if I had struck him with an iron rod. His name is Nathan. His daughter is an actress."

"No, Sandy. She's his brother's daughter."

Sandy looked at me and smiled, again that sideways little-girl smile. She said, "If you had a daughter, what name would you give her?"

"Name?" I repeated, perplexed. "A name that would hold her. If she were petite, I would call her

Nurit; if she were big, Hamutal. I would call a dark girl Yael—a gazelle in your language—in flight like the wind and as wondrous in beauty."

Sandy laughed. "And if she were none of those, but a small girl in whom greatness is hidden, the key being held by an adopting agency; dark, eyes bright, golden hair like mine, cheeks like apples, a brow sad as yours—what would you call her then?"

Sandy's eyes glowed with excitement when she finished speaking. The sun, expiring in the distance above the buildings of New York, which clamor their way into the sky, was swallowed in her eyes as in two green pools in some quiet land.

"I would call her Tamar," I said, drinking sunset from Sandy's eyes. "Tamar is a tall tree; its fruit, the date, is sweet and hard, its taste like quiet honey; its trunk mighty, having levels like a ladder, which can barely be climbed; its large branches are canopied, and open, like the fingers of the priest during the Yom Kippur prayer; its colors are the world: brown, red, yellow, green, blue, purple, black; the aspect of a proud and handsome prince, modest in character, shunning a great name, content; the savor of a loving woman, simple, feminine; its shadow in the desert, like a slave who commits himself to lifelong bondage, proclaims: this much I can do; beyond this I am bound by myself."

Sandy laughed and said: "Then Tamar is her name." I knew she was pleased.

Sandy resumed her story. "The pregnancy reached its final stage; the family was prepared for the infant. Though I didn't know who they were, I knew they would be good to the child. I had chosen them from a long list. He was a plasterer, amiable, not especially rich; she was warm and comfortable. I waited for the day when I would be rid of my burden and free to live like a human being, without shame, without a sham wedding ring, without a hundred and one questions: where is your husband, why don't we ever see him, when will he be back from his long trip . . . then, the understanding winks. Oh, I yearned to breathe the air of freedom —no more lies, fiction, deception. Yes, I waited. Fate waited with me, and though I wanted one thing, fate had something else in mind.

"I went to the hospital, drugged by pain, was put in a special room, given some sort of shot, and, in a delirious state, I told myself, 'This is it, it will soon be all over, the nightmare is coming to an end.' With all the pain, I was overcome by a simple and happy feeling and fell asleep. When I came to and looked around, I saw two women nursing their young. The nurse came in, her face smeared with a smile which extended from one ugly ear to the other (had there been a third ear it would have been equally ugly), saying festively, in her best Fourth of July voice, as if bugles were blaring, '*Miss* . . . you have a daughter now. I've never seen such a beautiful infant; she weighs eight and a half pounds and you look as much alike as two drops of water.' I said to her, too weak to scream, 'Don't tell me stories. I don't want to know about her.' I was, suddenly, overwhelmed by tears. The nurse tried to comfort me and then left. I cursed her with every muscle of my body, trying not to notice my two neighbors who were nursing their monkeys, and oohing and aahing at them.

"The nurse did not know my situation. The doctor had not told her about the adoption agency, etc. What did she do? She brought the baby to nurse. She said, 'Don't worry, many women lose themselves after giving birth. Nurse her a few times and your troubles will fly away.' She deposited the baby at my side and left the room. The baby was screeching a welcome to the world with all her might, flinging her arms as if she meant to jump through the window into the heart of the foul city below. The little creature clung to me. I took one look at her and began to tremble, as if I had just been given a name, as if I had just been born, as if my mother and father were both clutching me with love. One look and I was lost, drifting in a land of forbidden pleasure.

"The infant lay on my stomach. I put her to my breast, and with her tender lips, with simplicity and safety, she began to suck. Every drop of milk was a drop of love, frenzied love. This milk of mine began to pass through her body. I could hear it flowing through her veins, and with it went my self, all that I ever was or could become. From my body to my head the seething, sweet murmur of milk, from my head to my eyes which heard the pounding of my heart and opened its windows—from which tears began to flow, each one as big as my daughter's head. I knew I could not give her up, that I could never, never deprive myself of her, just as I could never surrender a limb of my body, my hidden dreams, my shame, my passion for punishment and remorse. My own baby, her head the size of a fist, her lips sweet as candy.

"I fought the agency steadily for two days— begged, promised, offered money, anything; they finally relented. I was wild with joy. I waited a few days longer, holding the baby, nursing her, never allowing her to be separated from me, and planning: how I would go back to Virginia, settle down, get a job and find a decent husband. I was absolutely charmed by her. The rest of the world was forgotten. The theories I had clung to during pregnancy had faded the first time I looked at her. A fatherless child . . . I would be father, mother, brothers, sisters, even a puppy for her to play with —and I taught myself to bark. Bow wow. This lovely miracle had chosen to happen to me, Sandy, who had always been nothing. I had made this handsome child, and when she was grown up, I told myself, we would link our arms and go gathering flowers with which to decorate our lives. Our bodies would adorn the world. We would be good and smiling. I would teach her to kneel in prayer, to be happy, to wear dresses like mine. We would pluck stars and arrange wreaths in our hair. How wonderful it will be, I told her, imagining she smiled. I am sure that she smiled, my little darling.

"On the seventh day I left the hospital. I did not as yet have any papers, but the man from the agency told me not to worry, that it would all work out, and even wished me good luck. I kissed him, also the nurse and the doctor—fool that I was. If it were possible, I would have kissed fate, and her flower sailor. Outside, the sun shimmered. The air was so clear, it could almost be touched. I hailed the taxi which was standing at the entrance, climbed into it, and before I realized what was happening the car heaved into motion, only to come to a sharp stop at the corner, where three men leaped into the seat at my side. The taxi was off again. I clutched the baby, in panic. It seemed to me that one of the men laughed. They seized me, slapped me, grabbed the child, and began to go. I pleaded, promising I would give myself to them if they wished, saying I had a rich father who would give them money; I cried, shrieked, hit, kicked, but it was no use. When we got to the park they stopped the car, pushed me out and disappeared.

"I was alone on the cold grass near the lake, where I cried until no more tears would come.

"I dug a little grave for her here and put a doll inside. She would love the doll, I know she would. It has green eyes that move, and lets out a sharp cry when you turn it upside down. She is three years old today."

Sandy's eyes were green as a cucumber sprinkled with dew. She had the form of a Greek statue, large and full. At home she loved to be naked.

Hers was a wondrous blend of reticence and abandon; her surrender soft . . . like a trained animal. She was a gentle evening breeze, rather like the mother of a sailor I knew, who dreamed of becoming a whore for him.

Sandy danced in a cabaret on Fifty-second Street. We didn't talk much. Our conversations were silence. She used to prance about the house, mincingly, nude, her step so light. We seldom went out, although we did sometimes go to the neighborhood movie or listen to music.

My wife was lost to me in the abyss of the city. She was still in the theatre, but I heard nothing about her. Even Uncle Nathan disappeared. It might be more precise to say in this case that it was I who disappeared. If I had formerly been an ill-tempered fugitive, finding refuge in ambition, at least I did see people, touch them, even take one to wife, converse and begin to seek myself in others' faces which, in contrast to my own, had substance. Now, I was without my wife, without the Zuckers, without Uncle Nathan. I changed apartments, gave up my telephone. Sandy and I lived secluded in a flat somewhere in the city which, if you wish, can bury you forever; no forest is as enclosed and as remote as any corner of this city.

Again, the unknown played an important role in shaping events, fate having strange manners. From out of this grave of ours on the fourth floor of a dilapidated house, I felt unfamiliar stirrings. It started with a restlessness I could not interpret, unspecified yearning. Sandy was good to me, gentle and simple. She was surprised when I suddenly began to tell her stories from the region of my childhood, from the lake of Galilee where my grandmother lived, the lots that filled Tel Aviv, the potatoes we roasted as youths, swearing allegiance to the Promised Land, to fight against the English oppression. Sandy, who came from Virginia, did not see what was special in these memories, the Jewish pathos in the yearning for a strip of land of our own. She knew nothing about the Arabs, about the British High Commissioner, about the Zionist Congresses, about the five socialist parties, about the War of Independence. She knew only that I was a foreigner, with no ties to anything, with no emotion for the past, that I had no friends, that I fled my country for reasons she could never fathom because, to her mind, the matter had no depth. Wandering, restless souls . . . why not come to this land, where everyone has fled, or was born to one who had fled? . . .

Sandy and I were both buried in the apartment, buried deep, linked to it by the fact that only in the grave did we feel a spark of life. We had met in a graveyard; now we were living in one, and when we died we would live in one.

She did not understand my longings, since she never longed for the decadence (according to her account) of childhood in Virginia: a red-headed mother, swallowing pills, peering through the window at a giant Negro showering half-naked . . .

The longings that emerged from my cemetery were fervent. I would walk down the street, watch people, feel revulsion. I knew I was seeking something. . . .

One day I saw a familiar face and, contrary to habit, I did not turn away. I knew this face, and the moment the person spoke, in Hebrew, my

heart began to throb. Perhaps this is what I had
been waiting for: for someone to turn to me in my
language, so that I could curse to the full, laugh
in the language I dream in, remember without the
need to translate, be what I was born to be—despite my will—in this place, where I was in consequence of my will. The fellow grabbed me, be-
stowed a friendly, almost crushing slap on my
back and declared with great relish, "You're from
Israel?"

Within a silver second, where I had been full,
now was empty yearning. I retorted, "If I am, so
what?"

He immediately produced a mammoth pencil
and inscribed on his heart in capital letters: SNOB.
He smiled again: "A pleasure to talk Hebrew in the
middle of New York, no?"

"If so, what are you doing here?"

"So it will be a pleasure. And what about you?"
he asked.

"I'm here for no reason," I told him. "I had an
urge to wander . . . here, there. The Wandering
Jew. . . ."

He made no move to interrupt and I became determined to pour out my soul. Everyone has a preying conscience. It has nothing to do with patriotism. Shame, yes. We all suffer the same beautiful shame. I felt myself reduced to babbling nonsense and took my leave.

I parted from him, only to be accosted by another.

"Have you heard?" he said. "The things that happen in this world."

"What's up?" I asked.

"They are giving the Germans atomic warheads," he said, and went his way.

Another comes limping by, on his arm a death-camp number. I am absorbed in my own reflections contemplating the condition of Israelis in New York. I consider these people, some of them the darlings, professional Israelis, deeply cherished by all. One in particular, a melancholy-eyed specimen born in Germany and trained in medicine, who finds himself in the spotlight of a New York café, clutching a ceramic drum, dressed in an allegedly Arab shirt, emitting frenzied sounds like the Arabs in a Hollywood movie and beating the drum to the "original" song of our patriarch Abraham driving his donkey.

To my surprise, the man from the death camp offered a response to my unspoken thoughts. He looked at me in astonishment and said, "I have nothing to say about Israel. New York is all right, a racing city that arrived long ago without knowing it. I sat in the death camp and watched an entire people enter, only to be carried out—corpses. I asked myself if it is my fate to be the Job of the death camps. What can anyone say? I had nothing to say. I had nothing to curse. It's terrible when there's nothing to curse. . . . They're giving them atom bombs now. They'll surely start another war. One that will destroy the whole world."

He turned to go. I asked his name.

"Job. And give me a dollar."

Again I meet a group of Israelis. Wherever I go I seem to find them, as if I had been standing in one spot and looking into facing mirrors. This time there is a girl.

She says, "So you're married to an actress."

"I was."

"What's her name?"

"Mira Zucker."

"Nathan Zucker's daughter?"

"He's her uncle."

"They say he's a prophet."

"I say: He tells the future."

"Nathan, the prophet, asks for you. He lives above us," the girl says. "He heard that I'm from Israel and asked where he could find you." She is well dressed, her jewelry is in good taste. "Why don't we see you with the other Israelis, in their coffee place?" she asks.

"I despise them. They shout like Bedouins in the desert, when actually they're too European to be that ridiculous."

"You're an idiot," she says. "The world loves us like that. I tell them all that we have no electricity, ride on camel back and live it up. We take off our shoes and dance until our feet give out."

I say to her, "Are there any camels left?"

She says, "Yes, Yosi saw one."

When I was a boy the caravans used to pass our window en route from Egypt to Syria. The Arabs used to sing: *Min hon le Beirut, mi hon le Beirut, ja-waz ya azabi. Bukra bidtak tmut, bukra bidtak tmut.* . . . They used to move so slowly, so ponderously. Today there is one camel in the zoo, and this girl with the bracelets smiles and sells him to the world.

"Let's go," I say, hating them too much to feel that we have anything in common, aware that I want to be with them only to suffer their company, a means of expiating a sin whose exact nature I no longer remember, though it has left a sharp impression. They exchange gossip about Hollywood personalities, discuss culture, read the yellow journals and denounce the void, the lack of values in American life.

We go together to Nathan, the prophet. He is glad to see me, embraces me, makes me sit down, serves tea. We talk about books, since he likes books and I like him. He tells me about my wife.

"As soon as she left you," he says, "she became successful. She seems to have found her way. Before, she was in conflict. You sat home and studied, read the morning papers, which to her was culture. She was on the stage. She wanted to be close to the creative world of the spirit, but actually she was in the midst of a materialistic world in which box-office success and publicity are supreme. She was torn. Now that she's left you she's found her way and she's happy."

"She was always stupid," I say.

"I don't know," Nathan answers. "There's a difference of opinion on that matter. You look bad," he adds, "and this worries me."

"That reminds me," I answer, "of the man who challenged a rival to a duel. His opponent said, 'Let's meet at five, in the park. Bring your pistol. I'll bring mine. Should I be late, don't wait. Just fire.' Someone fires at me at each street corner. I have appointments with everyone, which I never keep. Funny, no?"

Nathan, the prophet, studies me gravely. "Let's go out," he says.

We walk aimlessly in the empty night, and find ourselves not far from my place.

We were at the top of the steps, having already rung the bell. Sandy opened the door and stared in dismay at Uncle Nathan. They scrutinized each other closely, unable to remember where they had met. I said nothing.

Finally, she laughed. "You are the sad Jew."

He said, "You, the Sibyl. You divined my thoughts when you looked at me."

Closing the door and shoving them into the room, it was my turn to speak. "You are both angels. And now, my good angels, please come in and do be seated. You, the prophetess, make some coffee. You, the prophet, rest your crumbling bones. It was a long walk."

"I'm not tired," he said.

"Just the sight of a young girl and he feels strong."

Uncle Nathan blushed, sat down, emptied his pipe and filled it with fresh tobacco.

Sandy went to the kitchen and Uncle Nathan began to swamp me with questions.

"I met her," I told him, "through Mrs. Zucker."

He said, "Ah," as if nothing more need be said. "A wonderful girl," he exclaimed after a few minutes. "A beauty, what a woman, what grace. . . . Marry her, my fine young friend. If I were a few years younger, I would race you to City Hall. Marry her on the spot, and spend the rest of your life laughing."

I told him, "She hates me, lives here only because I remind her of her mother. Anyway, why don't you try it, that race to City Hall? Why don't you marry her? You would make her a good husband: the two of you, together, could wait for the Messiah."

"You're mad, Daan," he said. "If I were you . . ."

Sandy came in with a tray of coffee and we changed the subject, for it would be rude to speak of a woman in her presence as if she were an item in a store.

"Who said New York is a big city?" Sandy

chirped. "Seven million people, yet we meet again."

"It's because of Mrs. Zucker. Mrs. Zucker, of blessed memory . . ." Uncle Nathan said.

"You are truly a prophet," Sandy uttered in astonishment. "But how did you know?"

He was always in my house, proclaiming prophecies, engaging in long conversations. He invented a drug to renew virility and I helped him look for a buyer.

"This invention will make the old men crazy and me rich," he said, the gleam in his eye directed toward Sandy.

We used to play chess and drink cognac. Sandy would serve us, clean the table, empty the ashtrays, sit quietly in the corner looking out the window and singing to herself.

One day we waited for the Messiah. Uncle Nathan foresaw that He would come. He was due to arrive in the morning. The entire city waited. It was winter. People huddled together restively, ate quickly, snatched a shot in a bar and darted off, searching for an answer. They cried, shouted, moaned, waited, freezing in doorways. They hopped into taxis and gave the drivers made-up addresses, arriving at their destinations and finding no one to greet them. Wearily they went to sleep and woke up to disappointment. Not so we.

We were not disappointed. Morning came, the sun rose, big and beautiful, painted to look like a giant grapefruit. Uncle Nathan, the prophet, turned to me exultant. "The Messiah has come. We have been saved."

Sandy woke up and asked in alarm, "Did He come?"

"Yes," I answered, "He's here."

We continued our game. She slept on, peacefully.

That night, in celebration of these events, I got a little high, picked up Sandy and took her out. We went to Birdland, where we got drunk on Charlie Parker's sad crazy music, from there to Fifth Avenue to pound poems on the sidewalk Olivetti. We saw a musical play at the Bowery Follies. A fat woman danced, and a short man with a faded face told some faded stories. Half the audience was asleep, the other half drunk, all culled from the dregs of humanity sprawled on the sidewalks in that part of town. When we recovered the next morning we were lying near the river, in a close embrace, dirty and happy. A gang of truck drivers were railing at us, keeping up a steady banter to chase the morning chill.

We left town for the summer, swam in a lake, sunbathed, made pine-needle chains like the ones I used to make as a child in Israel. Sandy asked me if I would marry her. I refused. I told her I wouldn't like to lose another girl.

She cried and said, "I want to have children. I have been searching for my lost little girl. You have to marry me. I want a child so badly."

I comforted her, told her not to worry, that she was the only one who could make me happy. She wanted to be angry with me, but instead she looked at me with sly perception and declared, "You stay with me because I'm tall; I'm taller than you . . . that's why."

I threw a handful of sand at her. She screamed, then asked my forgiveness. "Will you ever marry me?" she asked.

"Why not?"

"Why not?" she echoed.

I repeated, "Why not? But why yes?"

"Why yes?" she mimicked. "Because——"

I didn't let her finish. I said: "That's a good reason." And the subject was closed.

At the end of the summer, in early September, when New York returned to its houses, once again filled its streets with frenzied tales, I began to teach again. At first the days were full: paperwork, adjustment. Soon I began to be troubled by ponderous thoughts. I was overcome by a sense of emptiness on a scale such as I had never known before. For the first time in my life I was bored.

Ten years I had been working toward a goal, and that goal brought boredom. People now approached me with respect, waiting for me to initiate conversations. They waited patiently to see their own faces veiled in infinite mystifications, whose significance they were determined to comprehend. I was afraid for myself.

"Up . . . up . . . up, above everything," a voice whispered.

"Am I not already there?" I asked aloud. This occurred in the university cafeteria. People smiled amiably, thinking to themselves: An absent-minded professor.

"No, no, higher," the voice whispered, taunting me. I tried to get rid of it, but it persisted, like a haunting melody when you are about to fall asleep. "Remember the fly," it said, "and the bird."

"Leave me alone," I implored. But it would not

yield. It tormented me, mocked me, turned playful.
I ran out of the cafeteria.

That night I rode out to the airport; but, seized
by the old excitement, I turned back immediately.
On the way I shot a stone into the cemetery. It
stirred up some old leaves. Mrs. Zucker, my
mother-in-law, lay there quietly, breathing the deep
smell of the flowers below.

I began to find fault in Sandy. Before long I
hated her, though she did nothing to incur this.
She had an unpleasant quality of "people together"
which I detested. She never argued. She was good,
agreeable. Yet her very being, how she smoked a
cigarette, folded the newspaper, her way of placing
her head between her hands and staring at me, a
long unswerving stare, acute and perceptive—these
small things provoked me.

You build an inside world, level upon level, like
ancient Jerusalem—whose every street is a world
in itself, and all the streets together one world. Every man has deeply rooted in his heart a scene, an
inner anguish from here, from there. In my case
this private world was built while running . . .

racing up a mountain, which continued to unfold before me, steep, overwhelming, until finally there was no more. A mountain with no peak. A mad dream in which I triumphed over nothing.

Man climbs because he is striving toward something; or because he is driven; or for love of the road. These are the three possibilities, none of which applied to me. In my heart of hearts I had no use for the academic life. Knowledge and learning for their own sake gave me no pleasure. The goal—achievement—was dull. I couldn't see what was driving me. I knew only that I felt deceived.

I began to ask questions. The voices continued to torment me. I understood their strange game with me. Although it was my own voice, it was wiser than I, yet offered no answers to my questions. The claim in Sandy's eyes, her femaleness, enclosing like a fortress, her complacent "I'm with you," which sometimes included a glimmering of under-standing—these were not the roots of my grievance.

It enraged me to be "understood" by Sandy, not because she was stupid, but because I thought that to be understood would mean not to be worthy of love. I had a sense of my own debasement, of my inner core as rotten, dim and sinister. My entire being was a mask, a prison in which the prisoner was forbidden to reveal himself. Sandy mustn't know, I told myself, discovering suddenly that her love was essential.

She was tall, lovely, healthy in spirit. I was slight, almost to the point of nonexistence, ridiculous, like the young goat in my mother-in-law's story: jump-ing, attempting to swallow the universe, at the same time regarded indulgently by a golden-haired girl of singular womanliness.

At about this point, very suddenly, at a time when my heart was sad and desolate, when time stood waiting for itself in the mirror, a faltering, road-weary knight whose soul seeks death—at this point my luck at the university began to advance rapidly. Colleagues came to consult with me. Important people valued my opinions. My lectures were published as a book, my theories made widely known. I was mentioned prominently in magazines. My name was placed close to the famous actresses, the popular singers who rank next to God in this land. I had a beautiful woman at home, a good job, honor—but in my heart: chaos, for I had been deceived.

I knew these things to happen: a man works hard, attains his destiny, meets disappointment. My case was somewhat different. I was placed high and praised because of a secret which could not be grasped by those who read the magazines and talked about me. Had I written a popular book, had I been the actress of whose body every man dreams. . . . But I was a mystery—a phantom. Those who mouthed my name with fervor knew not the reason for my honor.

The human has always offended me. When I was a child I was told: man is the cause of all things, the beauty of all things. I saw this same humanity as the undoing of my hopes. Virtue, expiating smiles, motherhood and fatherhood lauded in song, plain vulgarity, hearty eating, falling asleep as soon as one touched the pillow—all of these manners I deplored. I hoped to find a refuge in academic life. But the voices continued to whisper, to plague me. There was no out.

Sandy was a symbol of my confusion. If I were to yield to her gaze, to her devotion, to her help in ordering my life, this would mean surrender to the human in her, which is the human in all people—for if there is human in one, there is human in all. To this I could not accede. My mind was a whirl of conflicting programs, all constructed on fragments of logic.

The days that followed, devoid of logic and substance, were like flocks of ravens circling their prey. I used to seek each lost day in a night of terror dreams, yesterday having left no fragrance, no memory. One hundred times I would pinch myself to be sure I was not asleep, and even this was not proof. Dream fragments, like a dance at a ghost wedding in some children's story; knives flashing above me at all times; colored balls cast into the yard where I slept; or a strange prison in which I awoke screaming, this sometimes being transformed into a hospital where I was taken to a special room for questioning and could remember no more. My head was filled with songs, actually only the beginnings of songs, in constant motion, so that even if I awoke in the middle of the night they would be buzzing. With the songs there were sentences which stuck in my mind and repeated themselves endlessly: "An airplane to the end of the world, an airplane to the end of the world"; "Rise up, up, rise up"; "I've already risen, you're a fool, you're a fool"; "Auntie, Auntie, Auntie, tell us yes yes yes. . . ." I wanted to be King of Beauty in a shelter for the blind; to rise, rise. IDIOT.

Sandy was unchanged by my madness. She did not allow my delusions to rule either her or our "life together." She was still water in a surging tempest. When she woke up in the morning, she would slip out of bed, trying not to wake me, slink slowly, like a nimble cat, to the bathroom where she would make herself up like any other Southern girl, though living in sin with a madman, with me, in a northern city far from the grace and elegance of the languid South. Though she saw me as I was —a long time since I'd bought her a new dress— yet she would thread her way into our dingy bathroom, filled with old newspapers, its walls like the face of a gypsy, and spend a long time at her toilette. She would place an ointment in her armpits, eau de cologne behind her ears; with great care she would spread a bit of redness around her mouth, lick her lips like a delicate animal, as if she were in her mother's home in Virginia, maids and butlers in every corner of the vast plantation, the stir of horses being led from the stables for the hunt. This was Sandy. Even if her child had appeared out of its oblivion, she would have been incapable of rushing this ritual. She was quiet and like the Gibraltar of insurance fame.

Her stillness was, to me, as pigeons to the nerves of dogs. I would race out of bed, shout at her,

"What are you doing? Why didn't you wake me? How much time do you have to spend in the toilet?" As if I didn't know she paid no attention to the toilet. "Why do you bother with all that junk, making yourself up, when I don't even look at you? I suppose you've already made breakfast? . . . All this fussing, when right after breakfast you'll take a bath and it will all be undone."

She would never answer me. Rather than hurt me, she would send her laugh ringing through the room like little church bells and, though I wished to kill her, to slaughter her, to rip her limb from limb, I began to laugh too, all but choking, so that she ran to me and pounded my back to free the air that was caught in my throat.

"I'm going to drink some air, and by the time I'm back you'll be dressed, my elegant prince, and I'll make you breakfast," she said and left, smelling like a thousand flowers in the season of early winter rains.

I didn't know what to do with myself. "A good question," I said out loud, and the room laughed at my mischief. "If I am not for myself, who then?

. . . If I have something, then am I it?" I almost cried. "If I could have been anything but myself, or perhaps what I am *is* someone else? . . . Sandy will soon be back, and her cursed mothering impulse will feed me. I'll look at her, detesting her pleasure-gleaning face, her green-eyed daughter, her sailor whose brother I have become. I will hate her beauty, her height, her steadiness, her silent yielding; I will hate whatever follows, feel remorse because of it, and never be able to ask forgiveness."

Did I ask forgiveness of that little boy at Bet-Eshet? Of Mira? Of my mother or my father? I don't ask their forgiveness, and I'm not a man, nor even the insect I wanted to be with all the strength of my foolishness. Now that my soul is unsettled, I hear voices and buzzing, I sit all day and devise strange plans. . . .

I bought an ice-cream wagon, a small one, painted it shiny white and decorated it with my own drawings. On days when I wasn't teaching I stationed myself in the park at the entrance to the university and sold ice cream. Sandy begged me

not to do this. One by one I demolished her argu-
ments. "We all sell ourselves," I told her. "I need
more money. I'm famous now. What student will
pass up the chance to buy ice cream from me?"
She pleaded, but finally put on her red print blouse
and came out with me to sell ice cream.

The next day I was called in by the administra-
tion. They reasoned, urged, entreated me to re-
nounce my ice-cream wagon.

The university press had to contend with the
embarrassment of having just published my book,
with a most complimentary introduction by the
Dean. It was being prominently displayed in the
leading bookstores.

I was called to the university for a final interview. They had already urged Sandy to exert her
influence on me. She begged and pleaded. "What's
happened to you? What is eating your poor heart?"

At given moments, I am consumed by a sense
of debt, so that I knew I must answer her, without
knowing what to say. At such a moment I regret
all my actions without understanding why—like a
little boy who runs to his father, a stone poised in

his hand: "Daddy, unless you spank me I can't stop hitting Greenbaum's cat. . . ."

We sat facing each other, the bookcase lighted by the lamp, and I wanted to tell her everything. Instead, I began to throw books off the shelves, to hurl notebooks, diplomas Sandy had hung on the wall though they were waiting to be sent to my mother so she could hang them on *her* wall. I cursed the day of my birth. Knowing no higher source to curse, I cursed my birth, which I knew to be a singularly personal crisis, fraught with awesome guilt.

Sandy despaired and asked no more questions. "I love you, Daan. If you suffer, if there is pain in your heart, all of me cries, every limb of my body cries with you. If only I could help you. . . ."

The Dean and various other leaders of the institution were present. My ice-cream wagon stood beyond the gate, where it could be seen through the window, not idle in the midday sun, but glistening like a fresh wound. The Dean offered me a cigar and smiled paternally. He began to tap the table with his finger. The others present tapped with him, a chorus. They looked at me intently, and from time to time someone's gaze wandered through the window to my ice-cream wagon, its brightly painted colors a rainbow in the sun.

The Dean began. "What's happened to you, Daan?"

The others echoed, "Yes, what's happened to you, our fine young friend?"

"When you first began studying here, I already loved you. I had never seen, in all my days at this university, such devotion to studies and to work. My heart fell captive to your diligence. You were granted a position here, which is a big thing. When I finished my studies, years ago, I spent ten years as an assistant. Only then did I earn a full position. Then came your book, the research, the publicity.

Hundreds of letters were received here, celebrating your discoveries. We have always rejoiced with you. Your success was the success of the institution; your pride was ours, and I can say this in the name of all present."

The assembly nodded in full agreement.

"Suddenly, I receive word that you yawn in class. A student, whose name I shall not mention, tells me you devote an entire class to the folly of professors, the farce of teachers and pedagogues. Let us disregard this incident for the moment . . . The folly of youth. A man like you, young, impressionable, when something bothers him, has an impulse toward mischief; we can overlook this. But matters have gone from bad to worse, culminating in the ice-cream wagon. A respected instructor, boasting newly gained laurels, his first book bearing my own introduction, this man sells ice cream on the campus! What have you to say?"

"Yes, what have you to say?" the chorus echoed, and, as one, stopped tapping the table.

"I have nothing to say," I told them. "It is really very dreadful. You have deceived me, all of you.

My friends have deceived me, my mother and father have deceived me. Instead of telling me a single truth, they've led me on for ten years with vulgar lies. This is all I have to say, though this doesn't say much, since it probably is not too correct, and of course not altogether so. . . ."

The Dean became extremely agitated and trembled with rage. "What sort of drivel, what nonsense, how dare you? . . . Deceived? Deceived? What were you ever denied? You dare to speak of deception. . . . You child. . . . What right do you have to say these things?"

I said, "No right. Just so. Your Honor, Professors, did you ever climb a mountain that had no peak, open a package and find in place of the anticipated gift a small box, within it another, and another, in the end—nothing? No, you wouldn't understand. Because you are the salt of the earth, the silent fortress, the good men of science who dedicate their lives to the great ideal: knowledge. I, I have never cared what I do. I cared to reach the place where I would be able to do. . . . Now, I want to sell ice cream here. If you do not allow this, I intend to mount a barrel in the middle of the campus from which to lecture on the sex life of flies, or some similar topic."

At this point one of the assembly jumped up, pounded the table with all his might and shouted, "Enough. Either you apologize and recant, or you go. You are out of your mind." He spoke violently, looking with tenderness at his sore hand.

"I have found my mind," I shouted, and left the room.

I had wanted to apologize, to revive the excitement of the early days, to kiss their feet, to beg their pardon. But I got up and left. I didn't even want to cry.

Sandy was waiting for me at home with a gray face. They had called to say I was fired.

As soon as I received this information, I sold the wagon. I went home pleasantly occupied with rage, pain, thoughts of revenge. I held the university responsible for the shame that had befallen me. I was aware inwardly that I could blame no one—that this was no way for a man to live. This awareness did not temper the sweetness of my anger. In the dead of night I lay in bed wakeful, my mind brimming with hate.

I shut myself up in the house, spent hours at my desk, composing vituperative letters to individual professors. I indulged in personal attacks, analyses of their character, allegations against the university, its rules and procedures. I challenged everything I had learned during those ten agonizing years. The letters were stacked in piles on my desk. I never sent them.

Uncle Nathan continued to visit. My place was his second home. He would sit down in the corner and fill the room with smoke. "There is something to this," he remarked.

"There's nothing to it," I said, bristling.

"I know," he said. "You were afraid to give. You discovered something and were afraid. Like the fellow who discovered gunpowder."

"I didn't discover anything. They're nuts, and you know it."

"They know so much it makes them stupid," he said. "They'll come on bended knees to ask your forgiveness."

"But you really think they're right. Why do you defend me?"

"If I don't, who will? You're my friend," he said, and smiled benevolently.

My final barrier fell. "You're not my friend," I blurted out. "You never were. I have no friends, you know it. You must be Sandy's friend. You've got your eye on her. You've got a letch for Sandy and you ought to be ashamed of yourself."

"Stop it, Daan," he stammered, blushing with confusion. "I've said only the truth."

I left the room. He curled up in the chair. I could hear him crying softly.

Sandy was standing in front of the grocery, talking to someone. "Come with me," I said.

She mumbled a quick goodbye and followed, looking at me searchingly. She asked, "What happened?"

"What do you think happened?" I said angrily.

"I don't know," she answered, veiling the injury my coarse tone dealt her pride.

"If you don't know," I said, "why burden me with talk? Is this how you behaved with that handsome sailor, on whose behalf you lost your tongue, on whose stinking bed you landed horizontal only to wake from the swoon of terrible pleasure and find your daughter in a tree-shaded cemetery peopled by characters coming to commune with dead mothers-in-law?"

"Why do you say these things? What have I done to make you hate me so?" Her face was pale, her voice dim.

"I don't hate you," I told her. "I hate your kind, forbearing smile, your way with Uncle Nathan and his Messiah, his sunrise, his prophecies—that's it, your sympathy for that boor, that illiterate, that cad who has never in all his days earned a single penny!"

There were tears in her eyes. "You, preaching at Uncle Nathan? You ought to be ashamed."

"I stand before you, Sandy, totally shamed.

Every fiber of my body feels shame, and I am so ashamed, I can do nothing but stand begging your adorable person to pardon me, and then to be on your way. Perhaps to Uncle Nathan, to give him dinner. Remember, he has to be spoon-fed. You must open his mouth wide and, like with a baby, say: ye—ee—ss; then close his mouth for him. He might, God forbid, die of starvation. . . . Perhaps your sailor is in town again, looking for a hot night in the arms of a Southern belle, blonde, open-hearted, understanding. You could go back to the park together, or even to the apartment I've aban-doned. You could sleep with him there without freezing your behind as you would in the park. It's winter now, and you know how easy it is to get a cold. See . . . I do worry about you. If you'd care for some further amusement, why not tell him about me? Tell him we're from the same country; if he has a wife—who knows?—she might be my sis-ter, or my mother, or my Aunt Shlomit who should have married years ago. If he's from Jerusalem he can tell you about the quiet streets, the bell tower, a small café filled with a million noisemakers; if not, he might tell about Haifa, which is full of women like you, a port city, every one of its citizens provided with a cemetery where he can find the whore of death: blonde, green-eyed, brimming with tales of heartbreak."

"Stop! Stop!" Sandy shouted. "You're a child."

"I'm no child."

"You're an infant."

"Ten years I've slaved like a donkey," I said. "Not sleeping nights, filling thousands of pages, murdering unborn children, children already born and dead, fleeing from everything. I killed my wife's mother, I'm no infant, Sandy. Don't say I'm an infant—you spit right in my eye."

"I'm not spitting, Daan. I look at you with pain in my heart."

"Don't pity me, because you're so beautiful, so large, so full and so female."

"No, no, no. It's not that, you fool. I love you."

"You don't love me, my sweetheart. You love *him,* Uncle Nathan. Only him. Because he is pure, and his soul is clean as yours. Because he is sitting in my room now, waiting for you: 'Come, come

my lovely, our dances will circle . . . come, come
my lovely.' A great poet. He would write you the
Song of Songs if it had not already been written. . . .

"We are strange beings, Sandy. My entire life
had one objective: for you to meet Uncle Nathan,
for Uncle Nathan to meet you. Please understand
this. I fought in the war so we would have a state,
a state like all others with a government and parlia-
ment and army and navy of its own. A young man
joins this navy, becomes an officer, ships out to
New York, finds you, gives you a child, vanishes,
goes back to my far-off land. I find you because of
your child. Why am I in that place? Because of the
mother of my wife, killed through my sorcery,
whose grave is near the spot where you bury your
guilt, your shame, the memory of your dishonor.
We meet, two solitary creatures. Out of our sadness we come together. Through me, you find Uncle Nathan, who plagues your hidden conscience.
Sad old man, go to him."

She didn't say goodbye, simply turned and walked
away.

I walked aimlessly, thinking of Sandy and Uncle Nathan, how I had thrown them together. The idea obsessed me: tall, beautiful Sandy with Uncle Nathan. . . .

I went into a restaurant and called my wife, Mira. She was shocked to hear my voice. I asked for her father's phone number, which offended her. "Please," I said, "we have nothing to say to each other." She gave me the number.

I called Morris Zucker. I knew that he hated Uncle Nathan from way back, that he could not resist a scandal, that he had a penchant for the lurid. I told him Uncle Nathan was at my place, that if he would go there, he could witness a most remarkable scene. I described Sandy to him and threw a bottle of cognac into the story. I succeeded in arousing the old man to the point where he could no longer form coherent sentences. He insisted he wasn't interested, and that I should kindly go to hell.

A half hour later I saw him dash out of a taxi in front of my house and leap up the steps. I stood behind the door and watched him go in.

Sandy and Uncle Nathan were sitting on the bed. She was crying, demurely. Why don't they sleep together? I thought to myself, irritated.

I left, went to the river and threw up.

I don't know what happened in the days that followed. I darted from one place to another without discerning what was first and what was second —like the mercury that measures fever. I lingered everywhere at once, and nowhere did I not linger: the clinging odor of a small room in a cheap hotel whose place or shape I no longer recall, a travel office where a wall full of maps carried me to distant countries. I may have registered with one of those companies that hire labor to drain the Amazon swamps in Brazil, altering my plans upon learning that no Amazon had been seen there for four hundred years. Perhaps I did, after all, go, but never got there. Or, on the other hand, I may have arrived and returned, or never gone and never arrived; I really no longer know. Nor can I say how long it's been. If I did go, much time must have elapsed; if I did not go, much time must have elapsed, for in the latter case I must have imagined this exploit, and even the most fertile imaginations require some ground to stand on. I used to wander through the streets like a stray dog, not thinking even one entire thought. If one day a thought began to form, the fifth day found it still incomplete.

One day, on Broadway, at the point where it is no longer broad, where two trees grow—as in a Jewish joke, asking each other, "What are you doing here, this is New York," and answering, "Who are you that you ask, you yourself are a New York tree"— I met Uncle Nathan.

I didn't recognize him. He seemed to emerge from another world, from a previous life. He stopped me, a sweet indulgent smile on his face, and said, *"Shalom,"* as if he understood that the gropings of my heart transpire in Hebrew.

He spoke first. "I really shouldn't talk to you. But I want you to know that I've been searching

for you. I wouldn't abandon a brother, regard-
less. . . ."

I would have wished to embrace his honest
heartfelt pardon, had I known how to distinguish
what is true from what is not. I was seeking a hand
that would punish me, not in the manner of the
university, which had acted precisely as I had
wanted it to; rather as my mother used to, scolding
me for things I had no wish to be scolded for—but
what could one do with him? He was so full of
faith and delight, as if he had just seen a vision of
the rising sun, the bliss of the Messiah's coming.
This winning madman, his tongue lacquered with
sweetness, his untainted soul spread across his face
like a divine smile—while my body was wracked
with pain as if I had been lashed with a whip. I
realized my twofold punishment and, once again,
I was deceived. I seek one punishment, singular,
appropriate, beloved, and am granted another,
which I do not seek at all. Man has the right to
choose the punishment that suits him, I thought,
and thinking this, I knew I was nearing the end of
the road.

He said to me, "What made you do what you did?"

I told him, "Uncle Nathan the prophet, if you lived in the present rather than the future, where there is hope for the wicked, you would understand that I am not worthy of a single one of your words. Why don't you leave me and be on your way?"

"You mustn't talk that way," he said. "You look tired and wretched; why burden you with what once was? Let the past be the past. It is time to return to the world of the future, which began the instant I found you. What shall we do? Let's step into a restaurant, have a bite and talk. Nothing like conversation on a full stomach to kill the bitter taste of troubles."

He took me, all but dragged me, to Hassan, a Lebanese. Uncle Nathan knew I am mad about Oriental food, and Hassan's cooking had a good name. The place was small, neat, had clean white tablecloths. A picture of an Arab, mounted on a white horse, mustached and brandishing two swords, adorned the large wall.

We sat down, took the menu, made our choices.

I, reminded of my childhood, asked for *leben*. The Arab laughed at me and said: "It's *leben*, not yoghurt."

I said to him, "That's what I want, *leben* is what I want," recalling that as a child I used to eat *leben* every night and dream, as I licked the cup, that I would be *Leben* King and make *leben* in marvelous machines that would pasteurize the milk. The waiter (Hassan) stood a few yards away from the window which led to the kitchen, put his hand to his mouth as if it were a loud-speaker and called out in a big voice: "One *leben*, two *houmous*, one *kebab fantastique*, one *kussa*."

He wiped his hand on his apron, dashed into the kitchen, tarried there a while and shouted from inside, "Coming up, one *leben*, one *kebab fantastique*, one *kussa*, and some chick-peas on the house." Rushing back to the dining room, he arranged the plates on a large tray and brought them to us.

I laughed at this performance, and Uncle Nathan said, "Like in the Jewish proverb, all the world is a stage."

I said to Uncle Nathan: "How is *leben* made, do you know?"

"Boil two quarts of milk over a gentle fire, let it cool until you are able to count to ten with your finger in the milk, take a spoonful of *leben* from the day before and add it to the milk. Put it on the window sill, and the next day you have *leben*."

As we talked I began to recall, not so much the days as the nights, more particularly the dreams which tormented me. Nathan said to me, "Am I not a prophet, and is it not the prophet who is an expert in dreams? Tell me a dream."

I began to tell him, my memory clearing as I spoke, and, remembering, I was filled with fear. "I'm walking down a street, not far from the sea. Suddenly policemen come and arrest me. They take me to a prison, or a hospital, I can't remember. There I see three-foot spiders crossing the moldy walls of my room. I begin to hum children's songs, to wet my pants, to imagine I am a bee. Then I fall asleep.

"They call me to the office in the morning. A bespectacled inquisitor questions me:

" 'Name?'

" 'Daan.'

" 'Occupation?'

" 'I have none.' He looks at me sternly. I look back at him. 'It's true,' I say. 'I really have none. That's why I'm here. To start all over again. I've got a phobia. I'm terrified of high places—acrophobia.'

"He looks at me, this time with obvious satisfaction.

" 'Acrophobia,' he repeats.

" 'Right,' I say, pointing upward with my finger. 'Height is fearful; the more fearful, the more wonderful.'

" 'You were looking for something?' he asks.

" 'The sky.'

" 'You found it dull,' he says. I detect a trace of enthusiasm in his voice. 'You're afraid to die?'

" 'I am afraid,' I answer. I suddenly begin to shout, 'What's left for me now? My head is full of voices.'

" 'Yellow voices?' he asks.

" 'Yellow and black. How did you know voices have colors?'

" 'It's all part of one thing,' he says. 'People like you don't give up their freedom without a fight. You came here to imprison yourself, to be far from the sky, to be the only prisoner and the only guard.'

"There is a long pause. Then he concludes the interview: 'This is the place to find truth.' And I return to my room, a fantasy world, a world in miniature, wherein I am to seek the meaning of my life."

"One dream in a thousand," Uncle Nathan said. "Now tell me, why don't you ask about Sandy?"

I smiled at him. "I don't ask because if she's left and hasn't come back it's just as well, and there's no need to ask; if she hasn't left, it would be better if she were to go, and again there is no reason to ask; but now that you ask, I may as well: how is she? Has she had enough, and has she gone? Another thing, before you answer me: the entire dream, the one I told you, has a meaning I myself perceive. That I must begin anew, that there no longer is a past, so that even this restaurant, with its whiteness, its scent of the land of Israel, seems to me a dream. I no longer belong to memory, having burned all bridges; I never would have looked for you, yet we've met and are together. Still, when we have parted, we won't see each other again."

Uncle Nathan said, "I know, and Sandy knew too. She left you though she loves you still. Strange girl; she thinks that because you know her secret she is your lifelong slave. A sort of punishment she exacts from herself. Now, as for what you say, I will tell you a story from which you may learn something significant, today being story day. The dream you told me was not a dream at all, but a sort of reverie, a vision of what you would like to be. The terrible part is the revelation that for the merely mad there is a way out of the maze; therefore the dream. This prison is an asylum where all can be solved simply. The truth is that your mind is in balance, and you must find yourself a balanced way in this demented world. Ha-ha-ha. How alike we are, the longing to use madness as a rationale. . . . Yes, I did want to tell you a story, a sort of fantasy of myself, of you, of both of us. We have one soul, we are brothers more than relatives through Mira. Remember, at the funeral, when I laughed at Mr. Zucker who wanted to leap into the grave? You were angry at me and I loved you then. He really wanted to jump, but didn't know how to stage the action. They all wished he would jump, though they thought as you did that he didn't really mean to and was only acting. You, who mocked everything, didn't believe with all the fibers of your being that you were thinking straight and, though you wanted him to jump, at the very same moment you thought he would not, but would play the role until someone intervened. You stepped in, prevented chance from doing her part. How sweet and disarming you were then. Now, for my story.

"This happened to me, maybe to a friend . . . to someone. . . .

"When he was young," he began, "he yearned to be a comedian. More than anything he wanted to be laughed at. He told jokes and got no response. He worked as a tailor in a clothes factory for twenty years, all the while trying to find work in night clubs, radio, and so forth. Audiences sat fist-faced, not even the shadow of a smile, although the mention of his name could produce gales of laughter: he was a clown who never made anyone laugh.

"Once he climbed to the roof of a factory. The yard below was crowded with people eating their lunch. He shouted, 'Barbarians! I'm going to jump. I'm going to jump and be killed. Then you'll all be sorry.'

" 'Jump!' they shouted, 'Jump!' and broke out in rollicking laughter. A large crowd laughed for him. He jumped and was injured.

"When he recovered, he saw no reason not to repeat his successful 'act.' He would climb to the top of a high place, threaten, make the crowd laugh, and jump. His family finally brought him to an insane asylum. This was ten years ago.

"His world was a spider's web. Through his window the sun was blood-red. He waited for death.

One day he was allowed to go out. He talked to some people who were sitting under a tree. Everything he said made them laugh. At first he was frightened. He became depressed and returned to his solitary quarters.

"He was soon allowed to go out again. He told jokes. People laughed. He wove the jokes into monologues. He became a clown. At last he had found an audience. His public there laughed. They loved him. This success restored his health, but he stayed on.

"To have people laugh—for him there was no greater reward, because the people there were sad people . . . it was good to see them laugh. Millions were convulsed with laughter when Charlie Chaplin slipped on a banana peel. Here the bananas were embedded in their hearts. The cry laughed in their throats, the peel was deep inside. Clowns are the jewels of the world. . . . He was such a jewel.

"I will tell you one of his stories: 'I once saw a whippoorwill perched on a twig, whistling—oh so musically. His blackness glistening in the sunlight contained thousands of colors not in the rainbow. There was nothing in the world more delicate, more dazzling than this bird. With no warning at all, he alighted on my shoulder and relieved himself. I looked at him crossly. He returned to his place on the tree and began to chirp as he cleaned himself. I laughed. The bird saw me laughing, looked at me with scorn, spread its wings and took off, abashed and disappointed.' Understand?"

Uncle Nathan, having finished his story, was observing me closely. I lit a cigarette and looked straight ahead through the open window at the street, immersed in its bustle, in its affairs. I sat as time passed, hours, minutes, days, or years. . . . In the distance, out of a twilight, I heard the waiter shouting toward his empty kitchen, calling out various orders, dashing to the kitchen, announcing each dish, reappearing, and finally serving. Near me, two fat Arabs guzzled *arak*. An Israeli asked for *houmuz*. Hassan told him: "No, it's *houmous*. Not *houmuz*. Are you from Israel? I have a brother there."

"Are you Jewish?" the Israeli asked.

"Yes and no."

"What do you mean, yes and no?"

"Yes to you, and no to the two drinking *arak*. That's life, *habibi*. In this world everyone wants to make a buck."

In the interim, Uncle Nathan had risen, kissed my forehead and departed, without saying goodbye or taking leave of me. He had simply told his story and left. I felt as if steaming coffee were soaring up from the depths of my stomach and warming my veins. For the first time since that morning in the Kinneret when my grandmother bathed naked, I saw a happy image, tranquil, untroubled—this was my face reflected in the window which spreading darkness had made into a mirror.

I got up and left.

The rest was very simple. Wherever I turned I felt as if I were being pushed to face a mirror in which I saw myself, not knowing with certainty if it was I who was reflected. I began to ponder.

Why the disappointment, the despair when I received my appointment to the university? Why had this led me to the brink of madness? I had known such things to happen. A man conquers his field and instead of grappling with the gray problems which challenge him at the peak, he flits off in search of a new goal. But this did not answer my question, which in fact had no answer.

Again I secluded myself in my room, saw no one, hoping to find an answer through concentrated thought. But it was no use. My mind was muddled and out of touch with itself. I received a letter from home. My mother had heard I was in trouble and wrote me to come back.

My dear friend, I'm coming to the end now. The end is mine, belongs only to me. Still it is not because of it that I tell the entire story. The end was an accident. I am here. The fact that I have gone down so high, that I stand here alone, unknown, of no significance—this is chance.

There could have been ten other conclusions. God looks out from the other side of every road. There can therefore be many endings, although there is but one beginning. This is my beginning: rooms (I don't know why) in tall houses, gaping, imploring.

Morris Zucker, my father-in-law, is dead. He committed suicide. Uncle Nathan? He used to search the bathroom every night to see if anyone was hiding there. Once he found a thief and died of the shock. If it were not for his little ritual—he would still be alive. My place in the university has been filled by a young professor three years my junior, Dr. Veitel. He is very clever. His contributions will revolutionize the entire field.

For my part I have reached the point where it is necessary to think soberly. The same problem confronts me now as on that day in Bet-Eshet when I couldn't shoot at Amos. It is not true that my choice was made only once. I have actually chosen a hundred and one times. But I have learned one thing: that I used to think myself absurd, dwarfed, a segment of a swarming species, unable to swim like a fish, to be lovely as a flower, to soar like a fly—yet possessing the capacity for earnest self-knowledge.

Here I am, having crawled, tasted mud, been beaten, lived foolishly. Still I have regarded myself seriously. I am capable of contemplating myself without laughter. If this same belly-crawling creature can achieve self-awareness, then he is certainly significant. Because I am significant, I must be myself.

And I am here, on top of New York, despite everything, rather than because of it. I was walking through the city, thinking: it's time to go home. I seemed to see the sun of Israel in the distance, to smell the fresh vine blossoms.

I went so far as to consider various practical matters, such as buying a refrigerator, perhaps a car, a summer suit—as summer was not far off, and the sound man is one whose thoughts are with summer while his feet are still in spring. I even sent a letter home, announcing that I was on my way.

At the entrance to this building I noticed a sign:

> WANTED—*a guide, someone with good speech, articulate, who knows New York and can point out the sights from the observation roof of this skyscraper.*

I can't quite reconstruct it. All I know is that I applied, took my test and baffled the examiners with my exceptional intelligence. I still had the ticket to Israel in my pocket, but I took the job. Maybe this is the first time I have ever come home. I met myself at the halfway mark, between the clouds and the murky streets, alone, related to all things and remote.

I am here atop the tallest monument, erected to itself by the tallest city. This far we have soared —from here on, the winged world. This is man's realm—beyond it is the realm of the fly.

I can see the people, tiny, less than themselves, at the mercy of the traffic lights, and in the evening at seven, when the avenues are almost cleaned of people, I walk home. By the river I have my room, a few books, a small kitchen and cool, dreaming beauty under my window. I write sometimes and drink to myself, each day melting into another in dreary, beautiful succession. I like it this way.

Something in you may smile when you are so high and removed, not wanting to jump into the depths, as you descend upward.

Yoram Kaniuk, who is thirty-one years old, was born and educated in Israel. He has lived in New York since 1952. This is his first book.